Hotter Than Helen

by

Susan Wingate

The Bobby's Diner Series, Book 2

Hotter Than Helen

Cover Art by *Diana Carlile*

The Wild Rose Press, Inc.
PO Box 708
Adams Basin, NY 14410-0708
Visit us at www.thewildrosepress.com

Publishing History
First Edition, 2022
Trade Paperback ISBN 978-1-5092-4350-1
Digital ISBN 978-1-5092-4351-8

The Bobby's Diner Series, Book 2
Published in the United States of America

The day started like any other desert day spent in Sunnydale at the diner. Georgette Carlisle was surfing the internet and landed on a page about NASA slamming a rocket into the moon. She recalled the date. She recalled the pathetic fanfare—an event no one seemed to care about. It was only the moon, not Jupiter or Saturn. Since the 1970s, the moon somehow slid onto the backlist of newsworthiness by current twenty-first century standards.

The day coasted out of sight into flotsam of more noteworthy press like the inauguration of the first U.S. black president. The moon seemed to fade against today's bigger news, like the death of a famous movie star, whose news cycle would last for years. With an economic recession tumbling forward, sucking into it a pandemic swine flu outbreak and the escalation of the Afghanistan War, the world felt topsy-turvy.

And today, when the world seemed in so much turmoil, was the same day Georgette posted her first-ever monthly recipe contest on her favorite social media outlet. So when her old friend called, the moon's event, the war, and the economy all slid into other things less important at the moment, but things that would eventually change people's lives.

Dedication

To Bob, my forever.

Chapter 1

Sunnydale, Arizona, 2009

Steel shackles jangled at his ankles, sounding much like the ghost of Christmas future when he shuffled to a stop on the cold travertine floor.

Cabling, the kind used on bicycle locks, wrapped around his thin waist and angled off in a Y, snaring each of his wrists. He held his arms close to his stomach, monk-style as if praying, but unlike a monk, he held his head high, not down.

At a thick, red mahogany podium, the orange-clad prisoner stood next to a smaller-framed bailiff. The bailiff's hand cupped the man's elbow when someone called out, "All rise. The Honorable Judge Lindon."

The bailiff stepped back to the right, but the prisoner's eyes shifted left where his lawyer stepped up. The packed courtroom stood almost in unison.

Everyone watched as the judge walked in from a door along the courtroom wall where his desk sat. Sidling behind the wide bench, a dense desk spanned no less than eight feet long and three feet wide of the same rich mahogany as the podium where the orange-clad man stood.

The judge sat, pausing midway down to eye the prisoner over his black-rimmed reading glasses, sitting slowly before lifting the docket in front of him and reading from the papers.

He looked pissed.

Once settled, he slid his black leather and wood chair under the bench. Everyone else in the courtroom sat. Everyone except, of course, the prisoner and his lawyer.

The judge wasted no time. "Your sentence, sir…in light of this…" he hesitated briefly, rolling his hand in a circle as he spoke, then continued, "…this new information and these *errors*," he glared at the lawyer, "in allowing this new information from reaching the court at the time of your trial." The judge kept a hard scowl as he looked between both men but mostly at the man's attorney. "I have no other reasonable choice than to reduce said sentence to a lesser term, no more than two years beginning today." He slammed his gavel so abruptly he made the stumpy, tightly-combed, gray-haired court recorder jump. She looked up suddenly but went back to typing.

Judge Lindon continued to speak cautiously but with obvious anger and directed his emotions at the prisoner. His dark-lined eyes and the sharp angles of his cheekbones exaggerated the judge's mood. His mouth tight and his eyebrows in a hard V gave away his disgust for the restrained man standing in front of him. "You should thank your lawyer with some flowers or something for this one, Mr. Pinzer. He's pulled quite the acrobatic stunt. Maybe after his career as a lawyer, a career in the circus would be a fit for Mr. Ruckheimer."

His short but formidable lawyer, Wallace Ruckheimer, looked down at his feet over his fat belly and coughed into his fist. Zach Pinzer remained cool, not breaking a sweat, cracking a smile, or fluttering an eyelash. He simply stared, unswayed by Lindon's comments, just as his lawyer had instructed him.

No matter what, Zach, do not react. The judge can either hand down a lighter sentence or not. If he doesn't, we start the appeal process all over again, but this time with a higher, more difficult court.

He didn't need his lawyer to tell him not to react. Still, Pinzer remembered Ruckheimer's advice about not letting a muscle twitch. He tuned out the judge and spent the next few minutes lost in thought about the ineptitude of both the Pyles—the dead mayor and now his ridiculous, pathetic wife, a wimpy woman with no backbone, reneging on her part of the deal. The gall! A woman who spent her life in a balancing act, walking a tightrope and blaming others for her fate. Now on the run, she couldn't hide—not from him. He'd promised to find her, and he did. It was too easy, really. His man outside found her within a week of her taking off. She practically left a trail of crumbs. His man had replaced her in the deal already. Her leaving actually opened up a better plan of action, a much more devious plan. What was it people said? "When one door closes…"

Yeah.

Well, people would die. But who cared when he was dying in prison? No one.

He remembered the letter he shredded, the one where she stated she intended to back out of their deal. The strips of paper spilled onto the floor of his mind.

Of course, she would tuck her tail and dash back home to Sunnydale. The simple woman proved too predictable.

Pinzer stood there, not moving, barely breathing, until Lindon's gavel pounded once more against a hard block of oak, this time jolting Pinzer from his self-induced hypnotic state. He turned to his lawyer, and with his shackled hands, they shook.

Only the side of Pinzer's mouth, the side the judge couldn't see, tilted up ever so slightly into a half-smile. The bailiff stepped in again, his thin eyes glancing from the judge to the lawyer to Pinzer, then quickly leading Pinzer out toward a side door to a holding cell where he would await transportation back to the Florence State Penitentiary.

As they walked into a barren hall, the bailiff slipped a note into Pinzer's hand. Ruckheimer ignored them. Coughed into his fist again. His eyes ever watchful.

Unfolding the note, Pinzer read carefully so no one would see him.

He whispered to the bailiff. "Must I do everything myself?" He flipped his head to the lawyer who handed the bailiff a one-hundred-dollar bill. Ruckheimer looked around and slipped him the bill as if slipping a tip to a maître d'.

Even if things didn't work out exactly as planned, Pinzer knew he would still get what he wanted—Bobby's Diner. Operating from the Maricopa County Jail, where he expected to be transferred for the rest of his two years, Pinzer knew they could pull it off.

Chapter 2

The day started like any other desert day spent in Sunnydale at the diner. Georgette Carlisle was surfing the internet and landed on a page about NASA slamming a rocket into the moon. She recalled the date. She recalled the pathetic fanfare—an event no one seemed to care about. It was only the moon, not Jupiter or Saturn. Since the 1970s, the moon somehow slid onto the backlist of newsworthiness by current twenty-first century standards.

The day coasted out of sight into flotsam of more noteworthy press like the inauguration of the first U.S. black president. The moon seemed to fade against today's bigger news, like the death of a famous movie star, whose news cycle would last for years. With an economic recession tumbling forward, sucking into it a pandemic swine flu outbreak and the escalation of the Afghanistan War, the world felt topsy-turvy.

And today, when the world seemed in so much turmoil, was the same day Georgette posted her first-ever monthly recipe contest on her favorite social media outlet. So, when her old friend called, the moon's event, the war, and the economy all slid into other things less important at the moment but things that would eventually change people's lives.

Helen tried to hide the desperation in her voice. Georgette still heard it; call it intuition. Call it what you will. Georgette heard the tightness in her speech. Hundreds of miles south, she knew Helen was using her tiny smartphone. She pictured Helen holding it to her face, Helen's willowy jawline quivering as she spoke. Georgette knew Helen was somewhere outdoors. She remembered her mousy, lifeless hair so unruly in the wind around her face with a ballet hand grappling at the wispy, thin strands. Was she glancing around a busy Phoenix street corner? Were cars rushing past her in the city's hot train of traffic, bumper-to-bumper? And, as if Georgette were standing there with her, she imagined Helen's nervous frown bridging her forehead, causing a soft fold to form in the skin between her eyebrows. She imagined her glossy lips moving over each fractured word. The two women were complete opposites—in mind and body. Georgette also imagined her eyelashes trimmed with red skin, wet from recent tears.

Georgette knew Helen well. Always cloaked in something. Always scheming.

Even with this knowledge, she still trusted Helen, with reservations, of course. Georgette believed Helen, although slippery at times, would remain a true friend. The call startled Georgette.

A mounting bank of clouds buffeted the perimeter of Sunnydale's desert landscape and threatened action. It was early morning, a time when the diner's kitchen remained quiet in a soulful way, the way only early morning hours can produce. Except for chopping food on the butcher-block counter's soft wood, the place at this time remained perfectly peaceful.

She diced up a chunk of milk chocolate for a mousse she planned to serve as a special dessert for the evening shift. The cocoa scent attacked her nose and sent a pang of hunger like a knife into her gut.

First, the ringtone Georgette set for unknown callers, Beethoven's fifth, made her jump. Hearing those first disturbing, solemn four chords, *da da da dum,* and then the second set, the same but bolder, scarier, made her look around, wondering for a second what the sound was and where it came from until she figured out the ringing was coming from her purse. Seeing the display, Georgette realized Helen went from using her married name to using her maiden name again—*Wellen*. She quickly flipped open her phone.

"What?" she nearly screamed into the phone when Helen told her the news. "Oh my goodness, so soon? You'll be here tomorrow?

"No, that's wonderful, Helen. I've missed you so much. You'll stay with me. A spare room will be ready!"

Even after she'd returned from work, the conversation replayed in Georgette's ear. "Did you hear what I said, Gangster? Helen's comin' home."

The cat let out his usual breathy "yow" and jumped from the sofa where Georgette had removed her shoes, to his bowl. Sidling back to her, wrapping his tail around her ankles, letting out another sexy "yow," he walked back to his bowl—his way of letting Georgette know he wanted more.

"Yeah, you get down. You know Hawthorne doesn't like to find your hair on the sofa." He'd made it known that he wouldn't put up with pets on the furniture. "What? You're hungry again, Gangster? How 'bout some catnip? That'll settle you down."

Georgette pulled out the oregano-looking herbs and envisioned seeing Helen again, wondering if she had changed much in five years.

It was settled. Helen would stay with her for a couple of weeks until she found a suitable place of her own. Helen had sold the house where she lived after the mayor died. She left Sunnydale soon after for Seattle to pursue her dreams of becoming a writer.

Everyone loved Helen. Hawthorne would love her too. Georgette had already told Hawthorne nearly all the stories about the three of them after Bobby died. How Georgette and Vanessa, Bobby's ex-wife, God rest her soul, inherited the diner.

She always wondered about Bobby's decision about the diner. She figured Vanessa must have wondered too. Why he would do such a thing? Bobby didn't have a mean bone in his body, so Georgette was sure it couldn't have been out of some cruel inclination to pit the women against each other.

And after a while, even they began noticing their similarities. Both were strong, intelligent, and sometimes quick to react but always loving and kind. Well, most of the time they were kind. Hell, they even looked a bit like one another. Big, beautiful, red-haired southern gals. Of course, Georgette being from Georgia, her southern drawl differed from Van's Arizona-born dialect, sounding slower and longer.

It was almost like Bobby knew they would get along and manage his beloved diner better than he might ever have. And they did. Wasn't this the real reason Zach Pinzer ended up nearly destroying everything they had built?

Even now, she didn't understand why Pinzer wanted Bobby's Diner. Although, she did remember him ranting on about his idea of a perfect highway corridor and making it a new Sedona. Trashing their vegetable patch was nothing compared to him killing José, their beloved gardener and busboy, then nearly killing Roberta, Bobby's and Vanessa's daughter. She shook her head, unable to understand the criminal mind.

But he couldn't keep Vanessa and Georgette from prevailing, winning, and becoming as close a family as possible, especially being "once-wives" of Bobby's. It made her giggle, the term "once-wives." They'd probably be adding this new word to the latest Oxford Dictionary.

She remembered also telling Hawthorne about how she, Helen, and Vanessa sat after hours at the diner drinking wine and telling stories, laughing and crying, talking about the past, worrying about the future—all the things women are apt to do when they toss back a few cocktails together.

And she remembered telling Hawthorne about a letter Helen had mailed after she settled in Seattle, describing to him Helen's confession to her about Helen's feelings for Bobby before he died, but how Bobby never stepped one toe outside of their precious marriage. Qualities Georgette believed she spotted in Hawthorne—the second man she had dated since Bobby died.

The first man, Willy, fizzled out before anything really happened. Getting involved with someone so soon after losing Bobby wasn't something Georgette could let happen. She was also still grieving the loss of Vanessa to breast cancer.

The timing was off for Willy and her. However, sometimes, even now, since her engagement to Hawthorne, she found herself wistful about Willy. She

Susan Wingate

even went as far as wondering what life as a policemen's wife might be like. But it was high school thinking. She refused to allow herself these girlish and fickle ideas.

Wrenching her thoughts back to Hawthorne, she looked at her ring and thought of her fiancé. The diamond was so big it embarrassed her. He made quite a good living as a day trader and spoiled her with dinners out, bottles of champagne, and precious trinkets.

"Three carats, sweet girl," he'd said on one knee. "What d'ya say? Will you have me, honey?" He was such a romantic. Their whirlwind courtship lasted a long weekend, maybe. No more than seventy-two hours, she knew for certain. It felt like kismet. One day he moved to Sunnydale, and the next thing you know, Georgette and Hawthorne had become engaged to be married. It was all very quick and very romantic.

The proposal was like you'd expect to see in the movies.

She'd nearly knocked him over when she'd accepted. It was more of a tackle move on Georgette's part. She remembered saying "yes" as they clambered around on the floor, making love in the same spot.

Georgette felt herself blushing as she dumped a small pile of catnip next to Gangster's bowl. "There you go, kitty." Upon smelling the herb, Gangster rubbed his chin into it and then dropped on his side and rolled. "You nut." She loved her cat.

She looked toward Bobby's old office. The extra room. Nobody would care about the fact Helen hadn't succeeded as a writer. Nobody would care she was coming home. Anyway, who said she wouldn't be able to write in Sunnydale? Georgette made a mental note to suggest this very thing to Helen when she arrived. Helen would slip back into life in Sunnydale just fine.

And Georgette refused to find fault in Helen so long ago for trying to take Bobby away. Bobby was a good man, a true man. Attractive.

She knew nothing had happened between them. Actually, she understood Helen better because of it. Anyway, hadn't Georgette and Bobby done something similar to Vanessa? Who was she to judge Helen? Either way, it was water under the bridge. It was history.

She couldn't wait for Helen to meet Hawthorne.

****

Standing inside the doorframe of Bobby's office, she noticed her hips took up more than half of the door. Her denim capris ended at each thick, freckled calf. Her legs never tanned. She could live under a heat lamp, and she'd never tan. Her tennis shoes were her working shoes, easy on, easy off, with zero laces and the tongues lopping out like an old dog's.

Looking up, she ran a finger along the doorframe's dusty trim. The room needed a good cleaning before Helen arrived. She pulled back her strawberry curls and knotted them in a clip behind her head. She looked into the bucket on the floor next to her. Rags floated like dead bodies inside the frothy, steaming water.

A promise of new life and friendship within her home gave Georgette energy. Helen was like her sister. The thought of having her stay for a while felt like having family home again. She had spent too many days without family. Her future promised an abundance of family now with Roberta, Hawthorne, and now

Helen. Anyway, Georgette had intended to convert Bobby's office into a guest room.

Even from the door, the room smelled musty. A ray of sun angled across his desk and seemed to point to the lonely, unmade bed. As she stood looking in, she remembered the last time she'd opened this very door. It had been an entire summer, fall, and winter since she had gone into or out of the room. She told herself she kept it closed off in order to save money on heating or cooling. But the truth was she didn't want to deal with the nineteen years of memories she knew she would find when she finally rummaged through the boxes of Bobby's things.

Five years.

It had been five years since his death.

She walked to the big picture window and cranked it open. Immediately, air shifted through, allowing the dankness out and smells of early spring in—the hint of rain, rugosa roses mingling with cut grass. A forgotten wild honeysuckle blossomed, spilling its sweet smell into the room. The vine bordered the window like a Hallmark card. Its fragrance mixed in with the dry, pink desert silt reminded Georgette of her days as a child making mud pies. All of these elements created the very essence of springtime in the desert to Georgette.

Outside, a grackle trilled out a call to its mate, and a mourning dove hooted a sad falling lilt. After sprucing up the room, she needed to remember to refill the bird feeders; doing so would make the doves happy again.

She loved Bobby's office and had forgotten how much time she and her late husband had spent together in this room. She always did this remembering thing—

about the room, about Bobby, about a time so long ago yet seemed like yesterday. The images were so fresh in her heart.

Moments like this always stopped her, this feeling in the pit of her stomach nearly knocking her into a sitting position. Tears for Bobby weren't used up, far from it. It was only now she knew how to control her emotions. Emotions were simply something she had finally learned to deal with.

She still missed him so much. She missed Vanessa too. She chuckled, thinking how the three of them—Bobby, his ex-wife, and she—could've ever been friends, but they were the best of friends. Now, the one shining thing remaining was their wonderful stepdaughter, Roberta.

Roberta amazed Georgette every day by calling her, sending her emails, friending her on social media, and even following her Bobby's Diner fan page, something Roberta had talked Georgette into. She was Georgette's confidante, almost a daughter—almost. Once, she'd even told her, "Okay, you're close, but you're still not my mother, Georgie." She guessed this was the realm where they existed today—close but with reservations.

"Reservations." She giggled, thinking about the diner and Roberta all at the same time. It made her laugh out loud as she looked out the open window into the field where the deer canvassed. They were back again, for the flowers in bloom.

Gangster jumped onto the naked bed. She stroked his long calico fur. His claws dug in and out, deep into the mattress's ticking.

"Okay, Gangster. How about me and you get this

room ready for Helen?"

Chapter 3

"Please remind me why I decided to work here on my days off, will you, Georgie."

"Now, hon, it's not all that bad. Vanessa would be so proud. You can still buy her half, you know. I'll cut you a screamin' deal." She kidded Roberta, knowing the only reason she worked there was so she might hold on to something belonging to her mother. "Keep working that dough. It helps with stress."

The day started out with someone calling in sick, then someone else would be late, and the special for this evening had to be changed because the market didn't have prime rib today—Wednesday, their usual prime rib day—again, for the third week in a row.

"We're gonna have to call it 'Wait Until Next Wednesday' instead of 'Prime Rib Wednesday' if this keeps up."

"Well, if it ever reaches emergency levels, we can always send up a flare!" She giggled, thinking how a flare soaring over town might look to the people in Sunnydale—visitors and residents alike. She glanced at Roberta rolling and pushing on the pie dough. Her arms flexed, reminding Georgette of how Vanessa used to look.

"Gosh, honey. You look so much like your mom."

"Yeah, yeah. You always get nostalgic in the springtime." She grabbed a rolling pin without looking up. "Did you know that? That you get that way every spring?"

"Do I? I didn't, I guess." She cut into an onion. Fumes wafted up, hitting her in the nose. She sniffled. The fumes continued to bombard her senses, making her eyes water. While still holding the chef's knife, she bent her right wrist and blotted the corner of her eye.

"Oh good Lord, I didn't mean to make you cry," Roberta teased.

"You didn't!"

She didn't get Roberta's joke, which amused her. "Crybaby."

"You didn't make me cry! It's these damn onions." Roberta knew how easy it was to get Georgette riled.

"Crybaby."

Looking up at her, she finally understood Roberta had been teasing her. "Oh, you little fart." And then she threw a towel at her.

"So, how's Helen handling it back here?" Roberta asked her.

"She was tired from the bus ride and dumped a ton of luggage in her room, and even a shoebox full of letters or something in the cupboard out in the garage." The onions made her wipe her eyes again. "But she started looking for work yesterday."

"What kind of work is she looking for?"

"I don't know exactly. Probably something where she can write. She said she needed some time to think. I think she might go over to the Sunnydale Weekly and apply."

"Hmm." Roberta put her hands on her waist and then wiped them over her apron.

Georgette squinted, hoping to elicit more from her.

"What does *that* mean?"

"Oh, I don't know. Think about what? I mean, I guess, why didn't she ask you for a job? Or me? She could find something in my office. For God's sake, I'm the mayor. I have a little pull."

"Honey, don't take offense. I intended on broaching the subject of her coming to work with us here, anyway. Maybe she didn't want to be a burden by asking."

"We're her friends, Georgie. We are supposed to burden each other. It's what friends do to each other."

"You mean like what you're doing to me right now, asking me why someone else did something of which I cannot possibly answer?"

"Kind of like that, yeah." She looked up at Georgette. "It was five years ago last week."

Georgette let out a deep breath. "I know."

"I miss him."

"Me too, hon. More than you'll ever..." Georgette's words caught in her throat.

"Is it weird? I mean, is it strange that you've met someone else, that you're getting married?"

"He's amazing, Roberta. I loved your father so much. It's different with Hawthorne. I mean, I love him. Don't get me wrong. I trust him completely. He asked me if I wanted a prenuptial. I told him, 'Only if you do.' When he said he didn't, I knew I was safe with him." She set both hands down on the cutting table, still holding the knife. "Oh, I was hoping we could talk about this. It seems like a good time."

Georgette put down her knife and walked over to Roberta. Leaning against the counter where she made her pies, Georgette continued. "It is weird in a way.

Some days all I can do is think about your dad. Wish he was still alive." She paused and seemed to sink into the words. "He would want us to be happy, Roberta. Your dad was the most generous, sweetest guy in the world. He would want us to live." She waited and looked at Roberta, who hadn't yet looked into her eyes. "The problem is, he could never know how hard that might be for you and me." She patted Roberta on the arm and went back to prepping vegetables.

"The old fart." Roberta turned and walked into the bathroom.

After the door was closed, Georgette mumbled to herself. "The old fart, indeed."

Chapter 4

The sun was cresting over the Mojave, giving the long, cool desert morning shadows striped with crystalline rays the color of blood. The sky seemed to go on forever, not touching land for hundreds of miles off, shining iodine red and molten gold.

Hawthorne Biggs breathed in, smelling the light, sweet fragrance emanating from the prickly pear blossoms from cacti sitting in thorny clumps around each tee box. He stretched once with his golf club high over his head, gripping it in both hands and bending back ever so slightly, feeling the tug of muscles fighting him. Nothing was ever easy—getting old, earning a living, or golfing—nothing.

Diving his hand in and feeling the cool, rectangular metal plate, he skipped over it and instead pulled a long, shiny pine golf tee out of the pocket of his khaki pants with a gloved hand. The glove, the perfect match for his tan and black oxford golf shoes. He looked good today. He knew it. Every article of clothing new and matching, and with the latest set of Macgregor clubs, Hawthorne looked "country club."

Holding his driver in the pit of his right arm, he bent down and pressed the tee into the earth. Doing so always reminded him of shoving an ice pick into muscle, a piece of meat. Even the earth suffered when punctured. He looked up toward the sun, still in a squat, and smiled.

"It's gonna be a good day, Tanner." He stood tall, all six feet four inches of him, all two hundred twenty pounds. Like a wall, he stood, dwarfing the club and shooting Martin Tanner a knowing grin. "I'm gonna give you a butt whoopin' today, old buddy."

"What makes you think that, Biggs? You couldn't do beans to win in college. What makes you think you can beat me now?"

"Well, if I don't, I'm gonna wrap this club around your head. That's what makes me think so." He chortled to take the edge off his comment.

"Just tee off, for Chrissake, Biggs."

He pulled out a golf ball and gently balanced it on top of the tee. Standing up, he set his feet to address the ball, "Hello, ball."

He chuckled deep in his throat.

"Jeez. Hit the dang thing."

He knew his setup drove other golfers crazy, and Tanner was no different.

"Hit it! You're driving me nuts." Tanner grumbled.

Bigg's favorite straight line finally spoken, he turned to Tanner. "That's not a drive, buddy. That's a short putt."

"Screw you." Tanner grabbed the club like a baseball bat, acting as if he wanted to club his friend, and Hawthorne acted like he was scared, putting his arms in front of his face.

Then they both laughed it off, and Hawthorne turned back to the ball. He paused briefly this time, taking a long hard look at the green where the flag wagged soft in a morning breeze, the fairway doglegging to the right, some four hundred yards off.

"Yes, sir. A good day."

After turning his attention from his target, he addressed the ball, concentrating for a few seconds. Then he pulled the club back fast, cranking the club high behind him and swinging through in a swift, choppy motion down at the ground where the ball sat perched on its tee. He barely noticed lifting his eyes up before striking it. The club connected with a crack, sending the ball skewing off to the right, cutting off the dogleg, screaming straight for the pin and high over the barren desert floor, a floor contrasting vividly against the brilliant green fairways.

"Heavens to Betsy!" Hawthorne slammed his club head into the earth, denting the ground where it landed. The ball soared over saguaros, prickly pears, chollas, and a few barrel cacti growing in the light, sandy brown earth. As the ball spun through its route, both men noticed it pass over the desert and take a lucky bounce about fifty yards off the green and onto the fairway. He accidentally sliced the ball, and it turned out perfect for Hawthorne, like most things.

Hawthorne turned to Tanner. "Never lay up! That's my motto!" He bellowed out a hard, round laugh. It echoed over the undulating landscape of the fairway, pissing off Martin Tanner.

"I can't believe it!" Tanner was angry but still smiling.

"Believe it, son. And, Nimrod? What did I say about your language?" He tugged off his golf cap revealing a curly bush of salt and pepper hair across his tanned, almost red forehead. He scratched a spot near his hairline. "I told you it'd be a good day!"

"You lucky son of a bitch."

Hawthorne walked over smartly to the back of their golf cart and shoved the driver back into his bag like the killing thrust of a swordsman in a duel. "Take that!"

"How 'bout here. You'll never forget this hole."

"Yeah, here's good." He patted his right pocket, and after again tracing the edge of metal between his fingers, he pulled out the VIN plaque. He held it up for Tanner to see, his last piece of evidence tying him to the truck.

"Off the edge of the tee box next to the gold tee markers, we won't forget that."

"Very symbolic, Tanner. Nice touch."

The two men smiled at each other proudly.

Tanner backed off the flat, short grass into the thicker fringe of the teeing area and toed the ground. "How 'bout right here? He said 'hide it,' right? This seems like a good place to hide something…in the wide open."

Biggs looked around in a three-hundred-and-sixty-degree turn. "Perfect."

Bending down near Tanner's foot, he set the thin galvanized steel upright, sliding it back and forth, cutting with the edge of the metal through the grass until hitting dirt. Then, he jammed hard like a knife. The metal stopped halfway. He stood, placed his foot on the plate, pressed his full weight on it, and shoved it all the way into the ground.

"So, it's been drilled off the engine block?" Hawthorne asked.

Tanner nodded fast.

"Drilled out of the wheel wells?"

Tanner continued to nod as Biggs continued to question.

"And, we replaced the window shield and the trunk; did you check the trunk for the number anywhere in there?"

"Yep. All gone. The truck is clean."

"Well, then, this should do 'er."

"That should do 'er, boss."

"Let's finish this game, shall we?"

And, with the cockiness of a cartoon chipmunk, Tanner responded, "Let's shall!"

****

The thick planking of the rugged, raw pine table where they all sat shrunk in comparison to Hawthorne Biggs. A low growl of thunder bumped over the roof, causing the chandelier to jingle. Blinking tapers danced in the dim room, reflecting in each of their eyes, adding a hypnotic element to the evening.

Hawthorne daubed his mouth like a ranch hand. His big paw looked odd holding the gold-rimmed, beetle motif napkin. The napkin's fabric played an amusing opposite in his craggy, thick fingers. He set it down with a flourish, adding to the amusement.

"My goodness, woman," he bellowed. "You are the finest chef this side of the Salt River. And that's a mighty large expanse." Hawthorne laid his fork seductively onto his tongue and licked it clean.

His ample shoulders jiggled when he laughed. Hawthorne's physique challenged the size of the tree he was named after.

His tall, sturdy frame made him look like a man in charge. His chameleon eyes danced when he spoke, sliding from silver-blue to teal in a matter of seconds, depending on his mood. Teal meant he was happy. They shined daringly teal tonight.

But what most attracted Georgette to Hawthorne was his huge laugh. His laugh turned her head the first day they met at Bobby's Diner.

"Hawthorne. You exaggerate."

He shook his head fast, denying the accusation. "Now, wait one second, young lady. I'm not the only guest here tonight. What do you think of her cooking, Helen? Fabulous, right?"

Helen pulled back a misbehaving strand of hair behind her ear and nodded. "He's right, Georgette. This is wonderful." Her ears were her giveaway. They flushed pink when she felt uneasy. Georgette noticed how her ears always seemed to be trimmed in pink since her return. Something she hadn't remembered noticing before when Helen was married to Harold Pyle.

"You two." Georgette's emerald eyes glimmered in the candlelight.

"Pretty, too, wouldn't you say, Helen?"

"Now, Hawthorne. I'm only going so far with my compliments. It sounds like someone's smitten."

"Have you seen her ring?"

"Yes, Hawthorne. I've seen her ring." Helen rolled her eyes, and she and Georgette smiled at each other like sorority sisters.

"He just likes my food. He always tells me I'm pretty when I feed him."

"That's not true. I tell you you're pretty other times too."

"Yes, well, let's not go into that now, okay?" Her eyes opened wide for fear he'd let out some intimate detail.

"Oh, come on, honey. Let's talk dirty." He

snickered and shoveled in a heaping piece of salmon between his wide, smiling lips.

"You're awful," Georgette giggled.

"You both are awful." Helen shook her head and rolled her eyes. "Did Georgette tell you, Hawthorne?" Helen looked at Georgette, wide-eyed. "About the diner?"

Nudging her, she saw Georgette remembered.

"That's right! I've been so busy I almost forgot." Georgette set her glass down. "Hawthorne, it's wonderful news, really. Helen thinks she may want to buy into the diner." She smiled at Helen and then looked at Hawthorne for approval.

"You don't say." His eyes lightened.

"We do say. Plus, I've given Roberta every opportunity, but I think she's too busy at the mayor's office."

"Well, isn't that something? Don't you think we should've discussed it first?"

The women glanced at each other for the briefest second, then Helen dropped her eyes to her plate, and Georgette's eyes went to Hawthorne.

"Why, Hawthorne? You always said you would leave decisions about the diner up to me." Her arm rested on top of the table, and she leaned in on it toward him. "I think this is a fabulous idea."

Helen placed one hand on her stomach and rubbed. "I'm stuffed." She acted like she wanted to leave and slid her chair out a few inches.

Hawthorne stopped her.

"No. You're right. Of course, it's fabulous. Couldn't be anything but."

Helen shifted her eyes down from the two of them

to her glass when Hawthorne looked her way. She had just taken the last sip of her chardonnay when Hawthorne lifted the half-empty bottle from its chilly bucket and refilled her glass.

"Let's toast."

"Hawthorne, you're going to get me drunk."

"Now, wouldn't that be fun?"

He flashed a bright smile at Helen. His smile caused Helen to relax. She smiled back.

Georgette looked up. Both of their teeth grinning at each other and putting an exclamation point on his words. He flirted terribly with her and other women, even men sometimes. It was a fun personality trait about him. And, up until now, it hadn't ever irked her.

"I'd like another glass, too, Hawthorne."

"Of course, darling. We're toasting."

Helen looked back down to her dish. She poked food onto her fork and kept eating.

"Helen. Aren't you just the little wonder?" He spoke as he filled Georgette's glass. "Georgette was surprised to hear you were coming back to Sunnydale. Happy, but surprised. And now, this." They all exchanged a few restless glances and sips of wine. "I mean. You were in Seattle for a long time. Right? Why did you decide to come back here?"

"Seattle, although beautiful, Hawthorne, just didn't suit me."

"But, it's the literary capital of the U.S., isn't it? Timothy Egan once said of the region, it is 'militantly literary.' " Hawthorne always enjoyed showing people how much he knew about different subjects. "Or something to that effect."

"Now, Hawthorne. Don't pry. It's rude."

"But, I would think a writer like you would prefer it there. That's all."

"Yes. Yours are good points." She picked up her wine glass and sipped. Her brown eyes dimmed, and doubt coursed over her forehead. By the time she swallowed, she had recovered. The same strand of hair had loosened again and fallen by her cheek, framing her petite face, giving her normal, proper look a sexy quality. "I guess, Hawthorne, I just like the dry weather." She smiled, but in a way telling him the discussion was over.

Georgette had forgotten how good Helen was under pressure. She remembered her calmness when they spoke the night the mayor got into his fatal automobile accident. Even the mayor's death turned out to be something designed by Zach Pinzer.

"Well, good. That's good, Helen. You'll get lots of dry weather now."

"Helen? Don't listen to him. He's been nosy since the day we met. Always asking about things. At first, it bothered me, but then I realized he's just a sponge. Likes to know all sorts of things. For what? Who knows? Maybe he's thinking of writing a book too." Georgette glared at her fiancé.

"Now, there's an idea! Honey, it would be a love story…about you and me. Oh, and Helen, you too. I hate to leave people out."

"I bet you do." Helen was no amateur. She could dish it like a pro.

"Oh, ho ho! That's good, Helen."

"You two are horrible. Am I gonna have to separate you?"

"You just might, honey." He tipped his glass

toward Georgette. They clinked rims. Then he turned to
Helen with his glass raised still. "Right, Helen? We'll
need to be separated, right?"

Helen looked at Georgette like Hawthorne was
nuts, but she picked up her glass anyway. "You're
seriously marrying this guy, huh, Georgette?"

Her comment buckled Hawthorne. "Well, we
already have our engagement party set for this coming
weekend. A chance to kick up our heels, right, honey?"

The two women chuckled at how much fun he was
having. He took a big gulp of wine, then dug at the last
couple of bites on his plate. "I'm almost ready for
dessert! I bet it's ready too. I'm guessin' it's blueberry
brickle! I can smell it baking in the oven."

Georgette pushed away from the table. "You're
guessin', Hawthorne? He knows it's blueberry brickle.
It's his favorite, Helen." She grabbed his empty plate
and moved toward Helen, who was holding hers up.
"He asked me to make it."

"Do you need some help, Georgette?" Helen's
voice sounded strained, and she began to stand. As
Georgette was about to answer, to tell her she didn't
need any help, Hawthorne butted in.

"Helen, you're our guest! You keep your fanny in
that seat. I hate being all alone at the table. Georgette
can handle this anyway. Right, honey." It wasn't a
question. He didn't look up at Georgette for an answer
but, instead, placed his hand on Helen's arm, pressing
her down. When she sat again, he rubbed it gently.

"That's right, Helen. Hawthorne is right. Sit. I'll be
back in a sec."

Chapter 5

Looking inside a glass door, Helen stood chilling in the frozen food section of Sunnydale's corner market, the Sunnydale Food Center. She felt a blast of frosty air hit her nose. The scent of the cold gust reminded her of someone's dirty freezer. It was then she heard him.

"You want some Jell-O with that wiggle?"

The voice behind her made Helen turn around slowly, not sure if the comment was meant for her but still recognizing the deep bluster of his voice.

"Oh, Hawthorne." She stood up quickly and pawed at her hair. Her hands swept over her head down to the ends of her hair, and finally, pulling at the ends, she made a long tress hang over the curve of her right shoulder. "You're so bad."

She hadn't brushed her hair after jogging this morning, nor had she changed out of her clothes but instead went straight to the store in her T-shirt and sweats. Now, she wished she hadn't. Hawthorne wore an indigo cardigan slung over his shoulders. His eyes were a perfect match to the sweater's blue. The way he wore it reminded her of some college boy with the arms tied in front of his chest. The sweater's color set off his salt and pepper hair. His steely eyes disabled her. They didn't exude tenderness but rather intensity.

"Hello, Helen." Only one side of his mouth curved up.

"What are you doing here?" She continued to pat at her hair, trying to smooth it down.

"Picking up a couple things, you know. I still have my place." He bobbled his eyebrows up and down.

Helen leaned with one hand on the shopping cart as she spoke with him. Cold air gushed out and spilled around her ankles when the door fell closed.

"You're moving in with Georgette soon, right?"

"You're cold." He looked squarely at her breasts, then up to her face.

She looked down. Her nipples had gone stiff. She slapped her arms in front of her chest.

"Here, take my sweater." He began untying the sleeves around his neck.

Wrapping both arms tight around her, she refused. "It's okay. I'd swim in that thing. I just need to get out of this aisle. I'm freezing. It's the desert, and I'm freezing. Doesn't make sense, does it?" She looked away, turning to see if anyone else was near, then to the shelves across from the bank of freezers where they stood, then back at Hawthorne.

Seeing him there now, she understood how Georgette had fallen for this guy.

"You have fun the other night?" He was grinning at her the same way he had at dinner.

"At dinner?"

"Uh-huh, at dinner."

She nodded fast, exuding nerves, and then pulled her shirt together at the collar, making a tent in front of her and away from her chest to hide her breasts. Then she tried to angle her cart to the left, circling out from the area. Turning out of the aisle but missing the turn, she clipped the corner of Hawthorne's cart.

He didn't adjust for it, didn't budge. Pulling back again and finally maneuvering the metal shopping cart in a semicircle, she headed out.

Helen continued to talk with him as she pushed her cart away. "Oh, yes. Georgette and I always have a good time."

"You like her a lot, do you, Helen?"

"Of course. What an odd question, Hawthorne." Helen squinted at him. "She's my friend. Of course, I do," she repeated.

At the end of the aisle, she looked both ways as if in traffic. Seeing it clear, she continued left to the next bank of aisles. Hawthorne sped up to her, and they walked together with their carts side-by-side as they spoke.

"The only reason I'm sayin' is because maybe you'd like to stand for her. You know, at the wedding." The question stopped her. She looked up at him quickly to check his face and found something more than teasing in his eyes. His look didn't fit the question. She glanced away and felt her face flush red, go hot.

Being around him this morning and the other night made her uncomfortable. She couldn't gauge him. Then, a thought occurred to her, sending her mind whirling. Maybe he was flirting with her. It was just like Hawthorne—from what she knew of him anyway—to set people on a curve, make them feel unbalanced. It felt bad but, at the same time, titillated her. She kept looking at items on shelves as if she were still shopping.

"So, what do you say, Helen?"

"Well, only if she asks me." She paused. "What about Roberta?"

31

"Roberta has already agreed, but who says there can't be two standing for Georgie?"

"Well, no one, I guess. I mean, sure, yes, if she wants me to, I'll stand for her. Sure."

"Good, then. We'll see that it happens."

"Well, I need to get back. I need to find a few more things and get back." She angled her head down toward another aisle as they walked, as they talked. "See you, Hawthorne."

"Soon, Helen." He nodded and stopped following her.

She pushed away, leaving him behind, and then turned down the nearest aisle. She started to breathe hard, like delayed hyperventilation or something. She looked at her breasts. With each emphasized breath, she could clearly see her nipples through the T-shirt. She pressed the palms of her hands down on them—to flatten and soften them—to make them behave. However, sensing someone was watching her, she looked back. There he was. Hawthorne had both elbows resting on the handlebar of the cart, his chin perching on his hands. He was turned in her direction, just watching. When their eyes connected, he tipped his head and flickered a smile at her, making his lips twitch. She turned back fast, grabbing her shirt and tightly bunching it in front of her.

When she looked back again, he was pushing his cart past the end cap and out of sight.

Helen felt a warm tug in her crotch. She tightened her thighs, twisting one gently over the other, trying to make the warm sensation subside.

She couldn't believe what she was thinking. She couldn't believe she was feeling aroused by Hawthorne.

****

"He keeps me on my toes, that's for sure." Georgette had dragged the girls into the kitchen with her to talk about him. A blast of toasted nutty fragrance filled the room when she lifted open the tin of coffee.

"That coffee? Good lord, Georgie." Roberta said. "Hush. When will you stop about that kind of coffee?" Roberta smiled and let her talk.

"He likes to surprise me." Georgette continued. "I heard him the other day on the phone telling Martin it would be a huge shock for me. Maybe he sold his home at the golf course. He's just that way. Always something up his sleeve."

"I'm still not sure about him, Georgie."

"Oh Lord, Roberta," Helen interjected, "that's how you acted with Georgette. You've never been one to accept people readily. I think he's delicious." Helen stepped in closer to Georgette, reaching into a cupboard as she spoke to Roberta. She pulled out a bottle of Tums.

"Now, that's not true, Helen. And, even if I am a little guarded, well, I need to be." All the women stopped talking, and Helen and Georgette exchanged looks with each other.

"Rick is leaving."

"What!"

"Oh, not that way. He's leaving for Laughlin, some consulting thing, next week, I think, maybe after that. I don't know."

"Okay, girls. This is the deal. I brought you in here to talk about me and Hawthorne, not this." She paused at the sink while filling the glass coffee pot with water. "Isn't he gorgeous?" She giggled like a teenager.

"He is gorgeous, Georgette. I'm so jealous." Helen patted Georgette on the back.

"He's okay. Too old for me." Roberta joked. "Oh, you stop, now."

"I'm next." Helen dropped her arms. "It's my turn. I deserve a break, a go at the brass ring. I deserve a man like Hawthorne, too, Georgette."

She seemed almost mad, but Georgette felt it was just Helen acting.

"He's simply adorable," she added, which made Georgette smile.

Georgette turned her back on them, poured the water into the coffee maker, closed the lid, pressed it on, and turned to them both. "I know. I look at him and get, you know, aroused."

"Oh, gack, Georgie." Roberta put a finger in each ear. "La, la la, I can't hear you."

"You're such a baby." Georgette smiled and hugged her stepdaughter. "Come on. The boys are probably getting restless. That Martin sure is cute." She nudged Helen.

"He's okay. Kind of thin. I don't like thin much anymore." She looked down, acting embarrassed about how she may have sounded.

Georgette and Roberta both understood the reference to Helen's late husband, the mayor.

"Come on. Let's get back in there." Georgette avoided the subject and headed out of the kitchen.

As the women walked in, Rick walked up to Roberta quickly. "Rob, I was just about ready to come and get you."

Speaking to the small crowd, she said, "He can't live without me."

"Shut up."

"Oh, Rick. It's true. I remember you coming to the house once…"

"Okay, ladies. It's true. I'm nothing without her. Just a lousy piece of flesh."

"A nice piece of flesh, Rick." Roberta kissed his cheek, and before she could fight him, he flipped her around in a dip and kissed her hard on the neck. The theatrics made the group roar with laughter, especially Hawthorne.

"Oh, whoa there, stallion. Hold up now. Before you know it, this party will have turned into an orgy."

"Lord, Hawthorne. You're terrible."

Georgette giggled and snuck under his arm, giving him a hug on her way to the couch. She pushed the cat off and sat down. "Come sit by me, you gorgeous hunk of man."

"Oh, my dear girl. I do think you want a little action."

"Ick." Helen got out through a tumble of giggles. "He's so, so…"

"So amorous, Helen?" Hawthorne interjected on his own account.

"No, I was going to say *gross.*" She burst out laughing. "I don't know about you, but I don't want any stinking coffee. What I'd really like is another glass of champagne!"

"Oh, I was just dying for somebody to say that. Me too." Georgette jumped up from the couch, but Hawthorne pulled her down. She screamed and laughed. "Let me go, you big lug. You big, gorgeous lug." He kissed her to shut her up. She seemed to melt.

"Oh, please." Helen made a face like she'd eaten a

worm.

"Helen. If you want someone to kiss you, I can certainly help you out." When Martin Tanner spoke the words, the room hushed for a second. Roberta's hand covered her mouth. Hawthorne and Helen went quiet. Helen blushed. "I mean, I wouldn't want you to feel left out." His last words crushed everybody. With everyone laughing at once, no one could tell who laughed first.

"Oh, my." Helen held her hand to her chest. "Well, maybe we could talk a little first." Her comment made Hawthorne burst out laughing even harder, so hard he started to cough.

"How about some music?" Martin suggested. "We can talk while we dance."

Hawthorne continued to cough, making him jump up from the couch, worrying Georgette.

"Honey, you okay?"

"Oh, good gravy, George." He laughed through his coughing spell. "I'm dying." He raced toward the kitchen. "The cure? Champagne!" He disappeared but continued to entertain the rest of them by laughing so hard.

"Honey. Oh, jeez, honey. Turn up the music, for Chrissake!"

Chapter 6

As the four of them drove up and parked, the twinkling chili pepper lights trimming the eave, lining the doors, and wrapping around two saguaro cacti like candy canes gave Chavelo's a Christmassy feel amid the vast barren desert now turning dark around the restaurant. All four of them jumped out of Hawthorne's big, black truck, with as-of-yet custom license plates from Nevada reading BIGGS.

A distilled breeze skipped through the evening. A rare rain had been forecast, and it sure smelled like it. The air had cooled from the day by twenty-five degrees, and Georgette buttoned her thin, olive cotton cardigan. Seeing the buttons stressed across her chest, she tried to stretch out the sweater to hide the gaps between each button. She looked over at the others to see if they had noticed. They hadn't. Hawthorne and Martin Tanner seemed utterly consumed by Helen—thin, fragile Helen.

"This is new, isn't it, Georgette?"

"Brand spanking, Helen."

"I hope my stomach can handle Mexican food."

"Oh no, Helen. Should we go somewhere else?"

"Heavens, no. I'll just be careful." She held one hand on her stomach. "It's beautiful, isn't it? I love the landscaping. It fits in perfectly with the desert, doesn't it?"

"Nearly disappears," Georgette agreed, keeping her arms folded as she walked.

"It reminds me of yours and Bobby's house." Catching herself, seeing how the others quieted upon her comment, she said, "Oh, I mean, your place, Georgette. Sorry."

"It's okay, Helen. Bobby was a big part of that house. Hawthorne understands."

"Helen, I'm a big boy." Hawthorne smiled hard at her. "We're all adults. I honor Georgette's past, her husband, rest his soul." He turned to Tanner, who nodded.

"Thank you, honey."

"Of course." But when Hawthorne responded to Georgette, he looked at Helen.

The restaurant door swung open, and a man stood there, lean and tall, keeping it open with his body. His shoulders took up most of the width of the door. It was Willard Cleary, with his signature pencil wedged between his temple and his ear. A look he took on after he gave up smoking four years ago. For a while, he used the pencil like a pacifier for the real thing—twiddling it between his fingers, placing it in his mouth, a nervous habit he'd long since forgotten about, she guessed.

Georgette and he locked eyes. Willy's eyes, she'd always believed, were magnet eyes. In unison, the other three all seemed to say, "Evening, Police Chief," to him. Thankfully, no one noticed Willy and Georgette's connection. It was one thing she hadn't felt the need to tell Hawthorne. It was just one date, so keeping it under wraps didn't seem like dishonesty.

"Allow me, ladies, Biggs." Martin leaned in and

grabbed the door from Willy with all the flourish of the Marquis de Sade. Willard stepped out of the way, catching one last glance at Georgette, and then he walked off without speaking.

"Well, thank you, Martin." Helen tipped her head at him and flashed a smile. She raised her shoulders and wiggled through the door.

"You're welcome, you lovely piece of art."

Helen shook her head, rolled her eyes, and giggled at his comment. It was obvious the men were showboating on her account. Helen was eating up the attention.

The comment brought Georgette back into the group. "Good Lord, Martin. I can honestly say I've never heard that one before."

"Why, Georgette, when a man is surrounded with this much beauty at one time, he forgets he's not in an art museum." His lip ticked up at one edge, and he winked.

"I see. Is that how you feel too, Hawthorne?"

"Only when I look at you, Georgette. Only when I look at you." She felt his hand slide down along the curve of her back and rest on her rump. He grabbed a handful of her butt, moaned, and guided her through the door, his hand still on her rear end.

When Georgette saw Martin take notice, she objected.

"Hawthorne!" But she giggled too.

At the booth, both men began what sounded like an inquisition about Helen.

"Where were you born?"

"What is your favorite time to do your grocery shopping? What degree did you get again?"

Susan Wingate

"How long were you and the mayor married? How did your husband die again?"

"What kind of stories do you write?"

It bothered Georgette when she began to realize they were excluding her. She pulled Hawthorne's shoulder, gently leaning into him, and whispered, "I hate to sound like this, Hawthorne, but I kinda feel left out."

He darted a look at her, and his eyes softened. "Oh, sorry, honey. I just don't want Martin and Helen to feel at all uncomfortable." His whisper, while low, still boomed from his rugged voice.

Georgette nodded. She understood and sat back up. "Tell me, Martin, how did you and Hawthorne meet again?"

The men looked at each other. Martin's eyes squinted for the briefest of seconds.

"How about I tell the ladies, Martin," Hawthorne interjected.

"You always did tell it better."

"Oh, this sounds interesting," Helen added.

"It's very interesting, Helen, Georgette." Hawthorne made it a point to include his fiancée in the conversation. She nodded her delight at him and poked her fork at the bean burrito in front of her.

"We played football at USC. Did I ever mention that to you before, honey?"

"No. I don't believe so."

"Well, I played center 'cause I'm a big fellow, you know." He glanced quickly at Helen. "And this guy here, Mr. Martin Tanner, played wide receiver because he's so light on his feet."

"Like a dancer, they used to tell me," Martin added

to the story.

Everyone laughed.

"Hey, you guys..." Hawthorne flashed a daring smile.

Georgette looked over at Helen. She seemed to glow, and her look made Georgette happy beyond words. Helen even touched her diamond locket the way she did when she got embarrassed or excited. It was like her security blanket. Her face blushed.

"Now, see what you boys have done? You got Helen all in a dither."

Everyone laughed again.

Helen dabbed the sides of her mouth with the red cloth napkin.

"I have to say this is the most fun I've had in years. Really." She lifted her wine glass in a toast. "Here's to new and old friends."

The glasses clinked when they touched above the center of the table and when everyone was just about to take a sip, Martin grabbed Helen's arm for one final toast between the two of them.

"Here's to you, Helen. *Enchanté.*"

"Oh, my...*enchanté*, Martin." She looked over at Georgette and raised her eyebrows.

"*Enchanté*, no less." She giggled, and everyone joined her when she said the word again. "*Enchanté.*"

Chapter 7

"Helen, I'm back."

Gangster slipped inside, between her legs, before she almost shut the door on his tail. It was funny, but she thought she left him inside before leaving earlier in the morning. When she petted him, she noticed a light dew covering his fur. It was a rare day when desert air found moisture. She gazed back toward the sky. A series of long, thick, white clouds had grown. They were weak against the sun but still present. A wind sped through the door as if racing in to see what was going on inside, and Georgette followed it, closing the door behind her.

She and the cat both headed straight for the kitchen. The smell of fresh coffee wafted in the close quarters of its confines, and she looked over at the counter. There was still half a pot left.

Since Helen had returned, she'd pretty much taken to staying in her room or scooting off for long walks alone. She was gone a lot. And if she were home right now, she was being mighty quiet about it.

Georgette unzipped a can of Fancy Feast for the cat, scraped its foul contents into the bowl, and then set it onto the floor next to his water.

"Here you go, bud."

She reached over him up into the cupboard, fished out a mug, and poured herself a cup of coffee.

Gangster's heavy purring resounded through his nose and mouth while he masticated his food with utter purr-filled enjoyment. She bent down to pet his back.

"Aren't you glad Mommy came home early?"

She laughed quietly and watched as she caressed his back. Her eye was drawn instantly to her gorgeous engagement ring. Flexing her hand up, she held out her arm straight with the other hand on her chest. She still couldn't believe her luck in finding such a wonderful man.

When she turned toward the living room, there he was—Hawthorne. Standing there, big as life.

"Oh, Lord, Hawthorne. You scared the dickens out of me." That's when Helen walked out from behind him...in her bathrobe. Her hair was mussed, and her mouth looked red and swollen like she'd lost the war in a kissing match. She grabbed at the top of her robe.

"I'd better leave, Helen." His face turned ashy, and his eyes looked gray.

She nodded to him and smiled demurely. Then he looked at Georgette almost as an afterthought.

"Oh, Georgette, I'm sorry you had to find out like this." Helen's voice lacked any penitence like it had been going on for some time now. Helen had only been back two weeks.

Georgette scoured her mind as to when it might've started but became so flustered, her legs gave out. She felt herself lose balance backward only a few inches but landed hard against the counter. It was the only thing supporting her. Her body had reacted; her mind was grappling with the truth of what was happening in front of her.

Georgette hadn't yet gotten a word out.

Hawthorne touched Helen's shoulder to check if she was going to be okay in a shameless display of disloyalty.

"I'm fine," she said. "You go now. I'll call you later."

"Yes. She's fine." Georgette's words sounded insincere and sarcastic. But now she wondered if he would come over to check on her next—to see if she was okay too.

In what seemed like slow motion, Hawthorne turned back from Helen, tipped his head at Georgette, and cast his focus down to the floor. Then he turned to the door—one foot in front of the next, one, two, three, four—opening and walking through it, then closing it behind him. Not a word.

When the door clicked into place, Helen began to explain. "Georgette, we didn't plan for this to happen. It just happened."

"How convenient for you." Georgette pushed past her to try to get to her bedroom.

"Georgette, please!"

Helen's words stopped Georgette cold, but she didn't turn around. In fact, she didn't do anything. She just stood there.

"We kept bumping into each other."

Quickly Georgette snapped out the words. "Bumping? Is that what you call it?" Her sarcasm bit hard.

"Georgette, don't be vulgar!"

"Georgette, don't be vulgar? How about, 'Helen, don't be vulgar!' I invited you into my home. That does not mean you are free to sleep with my fiancé!"

"Georgette, I'm sorry. I don't know how it

happened."

"Well, then that makes you the stupidest woman alive!" She turned back around, continuing en route to her bedroom. Georgette's voice didn't pitch. It didn't waver. She spoke low and calm. She spoke in pain. "You will leave my home immediately. Get your...clothes on, Helen, pack your things and leave. Immediately."

Helen just stood there when Georgette finally looked at her. Tears streaked her face. She looked helpless—as always, helpless Helen. Always needing help! Always needing someone else. Always wanting someone else's husband.

It was strange how Helen despised her own late husband so much. They truly were cut from the same cloth.

"Immediately," Georgette reiterated. "Like in, now."

On that, she walked into her room and sat on the bed. Georgette could hear drawers opening and closing, the closet sliding open and shut again, the medicine cabinet being emptied of its contents, bathroom cupboards slamming, and, of course, she could hear Helen crying. It was soft. Then she heard her luggage roll off the carpeting onto the cold Saltillo tile and stop at the door. A couple of minutes passed before she heard the unmistakable sound of the front door opening and shutting.

Once she heard the car's engine turn over and Helen backing out to drive away, Georgette got up to check on Gangster and lock the door.

Helen's key sat next to a note folded in half. Georgette refused to read the note. Not now. Not until later, after she was gone forever, out of her life, out of town. When Helen was dead to her.

Georgette reminded herself to move the spare key she had outside in the potted plant. Both Hawthorne and Helen knew where Georgette kept the key. She didn't want any unexpected visitors.

She crumpled the pathetic note into her palm and walked back to her bedroom. After setting it on her dresser, she dropped the entire weight of her body onto the bed, sitting up only once to call for her cat, then dropping off into a quick and depressed sleep.

****

While falling in and out of her restless sleep, Georgette heard a reverberation of some elemental disturbance, maybe thunder along the outskirts of town. Or had she dreamed up the storm?

It was four hours later when the phone rang, waking her. The digital display brightly showed Hawthorne's cell phone number in her dark room.

Then a call came from Helen—well, she assumed the call came from Helen. The caller ID showed the Sunnydale Extended Stay Lodge. Georgette refused to answer either call.

The second call came quickly after the first from the hotel.

Then calls alternated between the hotel and Hawthorne's cell for an hour before finally stopping.

She didn't listen to their messages. She didn't delete them either. She would wait to deal with it later.

There was no way she wanted to speak to anyone. She felt utterly humiliated.

"Gangster? Come here, kitty." Georgette spoke through her sniffling. She sounded like she was surviving a ten-year-long cold. She hadn't stopped crying and could see no end in sight.

She let the damned phone ring on and off the rest of the evening. And after drinking a bottle of cabernet, Georgette slipped the diamond ring from her finger and laid it next to the crumpled note on her dresser. Then she went into the living room, where she fell asleep on the couch with her cat on her chest.

What had she been thinking, anyway? Who would want to marry a middle-aged woman?

Chapter 8

After reopening and rereading the message, he recrumpled the note, slamming it into his palm with his fist and wadding it up into a tight ball. Tossing it hard into the corner of his cell, Pinzer screamed.

"Aah!" Jumping to his feet, he pressed his face in between two iron bars. "I need a cigarette!" he yelled to anyone. "Hey, can anyone hear me?" He pressed his face harder against the bars. "Can anyone frickin' hear me?" he repeated. "I need a cigarette!"

The day guard, clad in a blue uniform, walked at an even, slow pace in front of Pinzer's cell. He stopped, standing with his shoulder in front of him, and looked straight down the hall. He patted a front pocket on his shirt, lifted the flap, and withdrew a cigarette. He slid the white rolled paper under his nose and breathed deeply as if he enjoyed it. He placed it between his lips, held it with all five fingers, and licked the butt with his tongue.

He patted the other front shirt pocket and this time withdrew a red plastic lighter. He flicked it, and a bright blue and yellow flame shot an inch high. Holding the flame to the end of the cigarette, he sucked in. Then he breathed in and held his breath for four hard beats of Pinzer's heart. He expelled a chalky cloud of pungent air into the hall, and it wafted in all directions, making Pinzer stand back an inch from the bars and sniff the air.

"Oh, that's good," the guard taunted, knowing cigarettes weren't allowed. He pushed his cap up off the front of his forehead and took in another deep breath. Again, he puffed out another peppery cloud of smoke, this time pissing off Pinzer, who leaned his shoulder against the bars.

"Nice. Very nice," was all he said. Then, the guard dropped the lit cigarette just outside Pinzer's cage on the floor about two feet away from the bars and, stepping over it, walked down the corridor.

Pinzer's arm proved just long enough to reach the cigarette. The butt end felt wet against his lips but dried out after finishing half of his smoke.

"Stupid Biggs." He sat back on his cot and stared at the mash of paper on the floor. He looked away. Thinking, he set his gaze at the ape in the cell directly across from him, staring at him but not seeing him.

"What are you staring at, dumbass?" The man yelled and stood up. Then, he attacked the cage holding him back. He ripped open the Velcro around his waistband and yanked his bottoms down. Wagging a red penis at him, he accused, "Is this what you want, lover boy? Is this it?"

Pinzer didn't react. Instead, he swapped the target of his gaze to the wall separating the animal from another cell next to him.

"Hey, dumbass!" the man said again, pulling up his pants and refastening them.

But Pinzer cared about the criminal as much as he cared about a cockroach. He was busy concentrating on his problem, the new issue about Biggs and the Pyle woman. The note stated Biggs had it "under control," but Pinzer doubted him now. Plus, in the note, he referred to himself as "we," as if he might not be working alone, something Pinzer had specifically instructed him to do.

"This is between you and me, only. It's my job. You work alone." He remembered their conversation when Biggs came to the prison. Biggs had assured him he would stay in line.

Now this.

Now, he'd gone and slept with Pyle's widow. Was everyone stupid? Biggs reasoned he'd had sex with her to make her vulnerable. She had finagled the Carlisle woman into giving her half the diner.

His body shook. He wiped his face with one hand and sucked again on his cigarette, nearly finishing it off in one breath. He dropped it under his foot and crushed the ember with his toe, twisting to extinguish it completely. He blew out a long, solemn stream of air, filling his eight-foot-by-eight-foot room, sitting like a ghost within it until it dissipated. *If this plan fizzled*, he thought but then gave up the worry. He sat forward on his bunk and considered the idea. Could his plans dissolve into oblivion? He couldn't lose the diner, that property or location, again. Wait. He adjusted his thinking again. He refused to lose it.

He stood, placed both hands on the bars, and stared at the man across from him.

The man looked up.

Pinzer glared into his eyes and, whispering the words so only he could hear them, said, *"You ever show me your dick again, you sick motherless freak, and I'll rip it off and feed it to you, rectally."* He didn't turn away. He pressed his glare harder at the man who let his hands fall from the caging. He stumbled back and hid deep into a corner, sinking into the darkness.

****

Georgette refused to close the diner. Not for this. Death, yes, but not for infidelity. Your fiancé screwing around with your friend? No way. The customers would have to deal with a few harsh words and some burnt meat. She'd been through worse. Nothing comes close to losing Bobby and then Vanessa. Losing Hawthorne to Helen? Well, it was just a weak excuse for pain. Anger poured from her thoughts as she chopped at a pile of mushrooms. She manifested scenarios of what she might say, "manifesting the awfulize," is what she liked to call how she was thinking. The awfulize distracted her into carelessness, and before she could move her hand, the knife landed on the tip of her left thumb, barely slicing the skin, like a paper cut, enough to hurt, but more than hurting her, it irritated her.

"Dammit!"

Danny, the busboy, jerked around from spraying off dishes to look at her and gunned water onto the wall and counter where he worked. "You okay, *Mees* Carlisle?"

"I cut my freakin' thumb." Danny turned back to his dishes. "Sorry, Danny."

"S'okay, *Mees* Carlisle." He kept his back turned.

She couldn't see his face, and it irked her.

"No big deal." Her words pressed like paste through her teeth, and she held her thumb, checking it to see if it would bleed. It didn't. She got lucky.

Danny shrugged his shoulders, keeping his focus on the sink, on his task.

"You know what?" She slammed the knife down

Susan Wingate

onto the wooden counter and walked over toward his work area. Her steps thudded to him at a quickened pace. He backed away as she approached. "Look, why don't you go out and get more plates. I'm sure there are some empties." She pulled the long hose from his hands. "I'll finish this."

"Yes, ma'am." Danny skipped out, almost knocking Roberta down on her way into the kitchen.

"Excuse me, Danny." She rolled her eyes. "He's in a hurry." Roberta directed the words at Georgette, who didn't turn around.

"Yep." Georgette lifted her wrist up and wiped her eyes.

"Okay. What's up? You've been a total bitch all week."

Georgette lifted her arm again and then wiped her nose on her sleeve. She refused to look at Roberta, not now.

"Answer me."

Georgette shook her head quickly, refusing.

"Did I do something to upset you?"

"Goodness!" Georgette let the sprayer fall into the sink. The sound clanked and echoed.

Roberta looked out from the swinging door to see if their customers had heard, then looked back at Georgette. "What is going on with you?" She walked over to her and spun her around by the shoulders until they were face to face. "What's...ohmyGod. Are you crying?" She pulled Georgette into her and held her. "OhmyGod, Georgie. What's happened? Tell me."

"It's Hawthorne."

Roberta pushed her back a few inches. Her face strained with her words. "Is he okay?"

Georgette rolled her eyes, pulled out of her hold, and turned back to the sink. She grabbed a smutty dish and angled a strong stream of water at it. The bits of food flew off under its power. "Oh, he's just fine." Her voice sounded deeper than usual and exuded a venomous tone.

Roberta's eyes flashed wide. She grabbed her left hand. "Where's your ring? What happened?" She pivoted Georgette around again by the hand and led her away from the sink. "You sit here on this stool, and you talk to me."

Georgette's body slumped over the metal work chair. She pulled out a used tissue from her pocket and wiped her nose, blowing once, wiping, and stuffing it back into the pocket of her apron.

"He's having an affair..." She didn't want the next words to come out; they just did, no matter how embarrassing they sounded. "With Helen."

"What the f—"

"Exactly."

"Helen and Hawthorne?" Her voice pitched up high when she said his name.

"Helen and Hawthorne." Georgette's body jerked as she chortled only once, hearing the humor. "Sounds cute, doesn't it?" she asked, not really meaning it.

"How do you know for sure?" Roberta asked.

"I came home. They were in her room. She was in a robe. She had swollen lips." She stood and pulled out the tissue again. Walking back to the sink, she wiped her nose. "You do the math."

"Holy Hernandez."

"I'm not in the mood for cute phrases, Rob. In fact, I'd love to curse a blue streak right now."

"Oh, Georgie. I'm so sorry."

"Yeah. Well, me too."

"Are you sure they were...doing it?"

"Jeez, Rob. They were doing it!"

"Did you see them...in the *act*?"

"Oh, good grief. No, Rob. Thank goodness. No."

"Well, then you really can't be sure..." She paused. "Can you?"

"Oh. I'm sure. Hawthorne said, 'Sorry you had to find out like this,' or something to the effect. How would you interpret it?"

Roberta turned away as if she were trying to locate something in the room. Her hand went to her mouth to cover it and then came back down. She wrapped her arms around her waist and kept looking at anything but Georgette.

"Don't worry. I'll be fine. Don't feel embarrassed for me, Rob. I don't think I could handle pity right now."

"Good Lord, George. That little slut."

****

"Where is she?" Hawthorne's voice boomed at the girl standing at the front of the restaurant, making patrons look up from their food. A glaring light streaking in from the linty-clouded sky behind him through the glass door silhouetted his big frame, deleting all color from him.

When she saw him walk in, Cammy, one of the waitresses, barely looked up, and without turning her body from the cash register, she pointed behind her toward the kitchen.

As Hawthorne moved past the cashier's station and away from the front door, his clothes, his face, and his hair all began to take on color, losing the grayness from outside's silhouette. He paused at the swinging door and glanced through the porthole. Tears streaked Georgette's face, and Roberta looked like she was trying to hold herself up with her arms wrapped around her waist. Roberta was speaking, but he couldn't quite catch her words. They hadn't yet noticed him looking through the window at them. When he pushed the door open enough to crack it, he heard Roberta stop at the word "slut." Then she turned around fast to see Hawthorne.

"Nice." He pushed opened the door fully and held it there.

Both women appeared startled by his presence. "What are you doing here?" Georgette asked and turned to the sink.

Roberta turned to face Hawthorne with her back protecting Georgette. "Well, don't you have balls the size of Jupiter?" Roberta challenged.

"Bigger," he said, challenging her back.

"You know, Hawthorne, this isn't a good time…"

"This is none of your concern, Roberta. Leave. I need to talk to Georgette."

Roberta put both of her hands behind her, feeling for Georgette. "It's up to you, George. I'll only leave if you want me to." She glared while she spoke.

Georgette turned and moved to the side of Roberta. "It's okay. I'll be fine. If I need you, I'll scream." She glowered at Hawthorne and wiped her hands on her apron. Then she untied it and slung it over the side of the sink. She pulled the rubber band out of her hair, smoothing it down and retying it. "I'll just scream." She squinted again at Hawthorne.

"You can leave, Roberta. Like she said, if she needs you, she'll scream."

His face looked older today, and Roberta felt herself smile. "I'll be right outside the door, Georgie."

"Mm-hmm." Georgette tipped her chin up and pointed it to the door. Roberta walked past Hawthorne as if he were infected, raising her hands so as not to touch any part of him.

Hawthorne rolled his eyes and waited to hear the whooshing of the door swinging as it closed.

"You have a ton of gall walking into my diner."

"Now, honey…"

"Please. If you say anything at all to me, please do not call me honey. You call me by my proper name. You treat me with at least some cordiality. Especially after having sex with one of my best friends." Her voice peaked, but she pulled it back, and it dwindled to normal by the end of the sentence.

"Georgette, now listen. I have some explaining to do. That's obvious. But, I…I…want you to know my feelings, Georgette. My feelings. For you. Have not…have not changed. Not one iota." He wiped at his brow, then added, "There. That's what I came here to say." He spoke as if reading from a script.

She leaned back against the sink and placed both hands on its railing. She looked down at her feet. He couldn't imagine what she would say next.

"Your feelings, you say. Haven't…changed?"

"Not one iota, hon…Georgette. Not one iota."

"You're saying…and please stop me if I'm getting this at all wrong. What you're saying is that you, Hawthorne Biggs, are still in love with me." She paused, and he nodded, quickly cracking a brief smile at her. So far, it hadn't gone so bad. Then she went on. "You can still love me?"

"Yes, dear. I do. I still love you."

"Oh, Hawthorne." She pushed off the sink and put her hands together in front of her as if she were praying. "You still love me? 'Cause I was beginning to wonder about your true feelings when I caught you with your Johnson inside Helen. You disgusting pig!"

His control slipped. His eyes burned.

"Look. It just happened. I didn't mean it to. It just did."

"How many times will it happen again? How many times has it happened in the past?"

"Never. Never to both. I got scared, George, real scared."

"Scared?"

"Yes."

"Of what?"

"Of us, of the commitment. Of forever. I guess. But scared. Scared to death. It was like stepping into the casket with a gun to my back."

"Good Lord, Hawthorne. Did you think we might talk about that?"

"I was scared you'd be upset."

"It seems you're just scared about nearly everything, aren't you?"

"When it comes to marriage, yes, I'm scared. Sorry if that offends you, George, but I'm just a man. I'm weak." He used all the lines he had been told to use. "I'm just a man. I'm not strong like you."

"Well, I don't want to be married to someone who is weaker than me."

"Baby...Georgette. How can I prove to you that

I'm sorry? It was a slip."

She put her hand on her mouth and looked up at him. She walked up to him, only a foot in front of him, and stood there. Her hands fell to her sides.

"Let me look in your eyes." She lifted up on her toes and squinted hard into his face. Her eyes flitted around his face, looking for lies. When she finished, she lowered herself back flat onto her feet and stood there silent, still staring. She wasn't sure if she wanted to forgive him or if he really deserved forgiveness.

"What?" He prodded.

"Don't talk. I'm thinking." She turned back to the sink.

He rolled his head but stopped when she turned back, resting against the sink again, and looked back at him.

"You'll have to atone."

"I'll atone."

"Tell me how."

"I'll, I'll...Son of a...I don't know." He threw his hands in the air, letting them land limply against his legs. "Why don't you tell me?"

She hooked her hands behind her onto the sink and waited for a minute. A minute too long for him.

"What?" he demanded.

Georgette, making him wait, rubbed a spot with her index finger under her nose but just above her lip. She turned around again to the sink and opened the cabinet below the basin, then, squatting down, pulled something from within the cabinet. It was a white plastic grocery bag with the handles knotted. She tossed it over into Hawthorne's stomach. "Well, for starters, you can take these sheets you two used and burn them."

Chapter 9

"Hell no, Roberta. I'm too old to have this sort of trouble." Georgette slammed her chopping knife hard into the butcher block. "He can go screw himself." She paused. "I am so sick of Sunnydale." Tears welled up in her eyes.

"Man, George. I know, but you can't just sell everything and split."

"Why not?" She pulled a white crumpled paper towel from inside the wrist of her sleeve, opened it, folded it in half, and wiped at her nose. "Why not?" she repeated. "I need a new perspective. A new life. I'm at this halfway point where I'm too old to start over but still young enough to want to. I'm letting the young side of me call the shots right now." She blew into the paper and wiped it back and forth across the base of her nose. "I'm letting the young me out for a spin. Good grief, I was a widow at forty, and I'm now divorced from my second marriage, before the wedding, at forty-five! That's not what I'd call a winning streak." She looked at the used paper towel and tossed it like a basketball into a garbage can. Roberta remained quiet while she went on her little tirade. "That's all. I'm done." She walked to the sink and ran the hot water, pumped some soap into her hands, and washed them. "You know what I mean? I'm just done. I'm tired and need to give myself a break." She pulled off two sheets of paper towel and dried her hands, then shoved the damp wad into her sleeve again for use on her nose later.

"I understand, Georgie. Believe me, I do, but I just don't see how running away is going to solve your problems here."

"Well, if I sell everything, then I won't have any more problems here."

"What about...," she crossed her arms and stood tall, "What about me, George? What about us?"

"Roberta. You're a grown woman. You have a husband. You don't need me."

"But I love you."

"I love you too, honey, but I have to do this for myself. I just have to." She sat with one foot up on the rung of the stool. "I just have to."

Roberta didn't need to stand there and beg. She needed a little space herself, so she turned away, shook her head, and pressed through the wooden swinging doors of the diner, walking out of the kitchen.

When the door swung back again, this time, it brought Cammy through with it.

"Order." She held up a ticket in her hand and slipped it into the hanging round, stainless steel order rack.

"Yep."

Cammy smiled. "I need a smoke."

"Take five. No more. Hurry up."

The waitress left through the back door of the diner. The sun was just about setting, and the sky looked like a baby's room with a light yellow, hazy blue sky and pink cotton candy clouds. They looked to be building heavier in the distance.

"Hey, Cammy."

The girl caught the door before it closed. "Yeah?"

"Will you prop the door open? It's too pretty outside." A knot lodged between her ears like she'd swallowed a rock. Her eyes burned.

"Sure." She squeezed the cigarette in between her lips and held the door with both hands, heaving it fully open and cranking down the industrial-grade doorstopper with her toe. "How's that work for ya?" When she spoke, the cigarette bounced with each syllable.

"Perfect. I can see perfectly now. Thanks, Cammy."

Georgette closed her eyes when she felt a cool breeze caress the inside of the kitchen, and she let out a deep sigh.

****

"So, have you talked to her yet?"

"Not since that day."

The Sunday paper still covered the couch where Georgette had been sitting right before Roberta stopped by. A pair of neon pink fluffy slippers with slots for each toe lay, one on top of the other, on the floor next to the sofa. She hadn't yet changed out of her sweats, nor had she brushed her teeth, combed her hair, eaten breakfast, or cleaned up the sink from last night's can of tomato soup. A half-eaten sleeve of crackers from a box of Ritz lay open on the speckled green granite countertop.

"I must look awful." Georgette flipped the remote over to turn off the TV. The screen flickered before zapping out.

"It's me. No worries." Roberta looked at her watch.

It was ten-twenty.

Looking into her own mug at a shallow pool of caramel-colored liquid and a few stray coffee grounds, Georgette asked Roberta, "Want some coffee?"

The tick, tick, ticking of Georgette's clock sounded behind them. "Sure."

Georgette pushed up off the couch, turned to the sound, and noticed Gangster at the door. His fur lifted from the wind that came through earlier. She shuffled, clad in thick cotton socks, to the U-shaped kitchen. Tying closed the sash of her cotton robe as she moved, she shuffled back, carrying the entire pot of coffee, and set it down onto a bright yellow tile trivet decorated with one single rooster in its center.

"Hold on, Gangster."

Holding her cup shoulder-high, Roberta let Georgette fill it.

The morning sunlight danced on the wall and shone through the French doors leading off to the patio. Gangster patted with both paws at the large door's pane, wanting in.

Georgette obediently walked over, opened the door, and let the cat indoors. "Wow. It's pretty out today."

"It's getting hot already."

Georgette shuffled back to where she had been sitting and fell back into the same spot. She snuggled her feet under her and grabbed her cup. "I haven't been out yet."

"No kidding."

"Shut up."

"Sorry."

They both sipped from their cups, looking at

nothing in particular, and *both* spoke at the same time.

"Look, Georgette—"

"Roberta, I signed with a real estate agent."

"You go first."

"Oh, sorry, you—"

"No, really—"

"You go…"

Georgette put one hand up in the air to stop and clamped her eyes shut. Then she put a finger to her mouth so Roberta wouldn't speak.

"Shhh." She dropped her hand and opened her eyes. She gave Roberta a steady stare until Georgette knew she wouldn't speak. "Let me speak. Please."

Roberta nodded and set her cup on the cocktail table. "I listed the diner with a realtor." She stopped abruptly and then gestured to her to speak.

"Can I talk now?"

"Please."

"You're acting hastily."

"That's your opinion."

"It's not an opinion. It's an observation. Your head isn't on straight."

"My head is fine."

"Have you even talked to Helen? Asked her what the hell she was thinking? Confronted her?"

"You know, she almost pulled the same thing with your father!"

"How is that supposed to make me feel, Georgette. Huh?"

"Sorry. I shouldn't have said that."

"No. You shouldn't have, but, again, your head's not on straight."

"Oh, man." She set her cup down on the floor next

to the couch, then put her legs down. "What am I doing?"

"You're acting crazy. It's normal for someone who just found her fiancé messing around with somebody else. Crazy."

"I have to get out of here."

"Well, that's fine. Leave. For a while. Take a week. Lord, Georgette, take two weeks, but don't sell the farm because of some stupid pig." She picked up her coffee again and sipped. "That's just plain stupid."

"Who will watch it?"

"The diner?" She looked over at Georgette, who nodded. "Who do you think?"

"You'd do that for me?"

"For a week!" She sipped again. "You come back after a week. If you need more time, then you stay at home and organize your tool shed or something, paint a bathroom." She set her cup back down. Georgette turned to her. As she listened to Roberta, Georgette watched as she locked both hands together to speak—a thing Roberta often did when she spoke officially as the mayor. "Look. I know you're sad. It's awful what he did to you. Helen's a tramp. Blah, blah, blah. But the same thing happens every day to all sorts of people. You move on." Roberta nodded with her last statement. A single bob of the head.

Georgette smiled, then she rubbed Roberta's arm. She leaned over to lay her head on Roberta's shoulder. With her head there, she couldn't help but notice the smell of her skin, a hint in her of something so offsetting but familiar, a perfect blending of Bobby and Vanessa. Suddenly, remembering them both, missing them like that, sent a jolt straight to her Adam's apple, but she swallowed it down, fighting against her emotions.

Roberta unlocked her fingers and grabbed Georgette around the waist with one arm. "You'll be fine. You got dealt a real crappy hand, but you'll be fine." She sniffled and pulled back. She dabbed a finger to the corner of each eye. "Look. You are the strongest woman I have ever met. Well, Mom was amazing, too, but Georgette, you two were equals. There's no doubt in my mind."

"Oh." Georgette's swollen eyes plated open as wide as possible. "Well, Roberta, my dear girl, I believe that might be the sweetest thing you've ever said to me."

"Yeah, well, if you tell anyone. I'll deny it." She laughed once.

"I guess I have my work cut out for me."

"I guess." Roberta concurred.

"Okay, so, first thing. Call the realtor and cancel my listing."

"Yep."

"Second. Take a cruise. Meet some tan muscle boy; let him help me lift weights."

"Okay. Stop. Gross."

"I'm just talkin' a little exercise, Roberta. You know, squeeze and tug and squeeze and…"

"Gross. I'm leaving."

"No, don't. I'm joking, but I do need to get out for a week, like you said." She nodded and picked up her coffee from the floor. "A cruise? Kinda sounds nice, doesn't it?"

"You left out something."

"What's that?"

"You need to call Helen."

"No."

"Georgette. If for no other reason than to let her know how she ruined things for you."

"I'm sure she knows without me speaking with her."

"You will always wish you had told her. It will gnaw at you until you die."

Georgette looked at Roberta. She wasn't sure if she was speaking from her own personal feelings or if it was something Vanessa had said one time in her past. Their eyes locked. She didn't need to know. She could see the truth behind her words and heard Vanessa's pain speaking to her, even through Roberta's eyes.

"I will try. That's all I can say."

Roberta patted her knee and rose. She looked at Georgette, then behind her.

"Your cat wants back out."

"That cat is my exercise, you mean." As Georgette rose, Roberta held out a hand to help. "Thanks, honey." She grabbed her around the waist and hugged her. "For everything. For talking me down."

"Anytime." Then she pulled back, and Georgette walked to the French doors.

"Go, you little monster." She closed the door behind him.

"Just so you know...I mean, if you hear." Roberta ran a hand through her hair. "I've been trying to reach Helen myself."

"Why?"

"I have my reasons. Anyway, she hasn't returned any of my calls."

"The chicken."

"Yeah, well. If you talk to her, tell her I need to talk with her too."

"This is my fight, Roberta."

"Yes, it is. You're my only family outside of Rick, and you know what? I get to have my say as well. Just tell her I'm next."

"Okay, dear. But you really don't have to."

"Oh, but, Georgie...I really do."

Chapter 10

Helen saw Georgette's car at the diner and knew she wouldn't be home.

Helen jabbed her fingers into the soil of the planter, searching. Georgette had left the extra key in the pot just like she had before Helen moved away from Sunnydale, just like when she moved back.

Helen wiped the peat and soil from her hands. Her gaze darted behind her, across the street, and down the road to see if anyone was watching. Shaking the last few crumbs of dirt off, she angled the key into the lock. When she looked down at her hands as they moved, she could see a line of swollen skin under her eyelids. Her cheeks were thick from the night before, a night she'd spent crying. Her skin flushed beet red. The color had not subsided even after taking a cold shower at the hotel. She had thrown on her clothing and hadn't the time or energy to blow-dry her hair, causing a reaction of electrostatic sprigs to dance around her face and stick to her skin like cobwebs, reminding her of Medusa and her snake-laden skull.

She flopped her sunglasses from on top of her head to back down over her eyes. After unlocking the door, Helen jammed the key back again into the plant's soil and slipped inside Georgette's house.

As usual, hearing the door slam and the lock flipping into position, Gangster came running into the kitchen. He sat on the floor, whipping his tail back and forth and watching Helen scurry around.

She trotted to the cupboard where Georgette kept her antacid. She popped two, three, and then four into her mouth and munched them fast, swallowing them and gulping down a cold-water chaser. This whole mess with Pinzer and Biggs had her stomach tied in knots for weeks.

Gangster whispered out a raspy yowl. She wiped her mouth with her arm, looking at Gangster, her mind spinning in all directions. She noticed him but didn't—all at the same time.

"Hey, cat." Her words were as brisk as her steps past him. She practically leaped over him.

Gangster ambled a few steps after Helen but stopped in the living room, where he jumped up on the couch and began washing his face.

A thick lump bubbled up into her throat on the way to her room—the guest room, she corrected herself.

Flipping through papers on the desk, she found a blank piece to write on.

Swallowing hard, trying to make the knot in her throat subside, she grabbed at her stomach, sat down, and flung open a drawer. Finding a pen, she pushed the drawer back in hard, causing it to sound like a slap across the face. Then she rubbed her fist into her gut. The pain had intensified over the past week since leaving Georgette's and getting a room at the hotel.

After writing the beginning, after starting her letter to Georgette off with an apology, she began crying again. The embarrassment had started with her own husband. Why couldn't she shake his ghost? He still haunted her.

She finished the note explaining everything—how Pinzer contacted her in Seattle out of the blue and how the idea seemed almost too simple, too perfect. But after realizing she could slip back into life in Sunnydale, how nothing of his plan needed to go through, how she didn't need Pinzer at all, she decided she would just back out. She and Georgette could just as easily have become business partners. There really would be no reason to "dispose of" anyone. Life could just go on as if Pinzer had never contacted her.

But then Hawthorne happened. They became involved, and she unraveled when he exposed his true intentions.

She laid the letter out clearly, so when Georgette came to clear her things from the room, she would find it and understand how Helen had changed her mind about the whole thing. How she was merely a dupe in Pinzer's scheme.

But as she began to tongue the flap of the envelope, she heard the rumbling sound of an engine. She heard it pull into the driveway, then stop.

Helen jumped at the silence the truck left when the engine died. Still gripping the envelope, she folded the lip inside itself.

Peering out from the hall, she spotted Hawthorne's truck. He'd found her.

Helen heard two doors slam, then men's voices nearing the house.

She couldn't remember if she'd relocked the kitchen door.

She peeked out into the hall. Except for Gangster sitting by the door, her path to the bathroom was clear. She slipped across the hall and ducked inside. The cat slipped in behind her. Helen didn't notice he'd followed her. Then she clicked the door locked. The bathroom had a second door leading directly into the garage.

The men pounded at the front door. Then it was quiet.

Then she heard the door open. And heard it slamming shut.

Trying to make no noise, she sneaked open the garage door and hoped they wouldn't find her in there. But as the thought occurred, Hawthorne spoke just outside the bathroom in the hallway.

"Helen, honey. Don't make this difficult. Open the freaking door." He jiggled the bathroom doorknob. Gangster wrapped around her legs and jumped.

Then she heard their footsteps pad away. They were walking into her old room.

She looked down at the envelope in her sweaty palm. Turning the knob slowly, making no sound, Helen opened the door, letting the cat follow her as she crept into the garage.

"Check the door again," his voice boomed. They had returned to the bathroom. She could hear the bathroom door jiggling again.

He started talking to her. "I know you're in there, Helen. Your car's outside." He said it in a singsongy manner, taunting her; then she heard the sound of something being inserted into the small hole of the doorknob in an effort to unlock it.

Upon entering the garage, the darkness subsumed all shape and form. She lost track of the cat. She could barely see her own hands. But she couldn't think about the stupid cat, not now. She had to worry about saving her own skin.

Inside the pitch-black emptiness, she groped around until her eyes adjusted as the men banged against the bathroom door, yelling to her about breaking it down. After feeling around for the cabinet, the one she stored her old papers in, she opened it and slipped her note inside, then closed it.

Unable to see for certain, something matted and unfamiliar brushed across her hand gently. She recoiled and gasped. Nothing happened, only her nerves sending a splitting chill through her spine.

She slipped the loop of the combination lock through the cabinet's latch. Everything else felt like dark water. She had no baseline of where she was because of utter murkiness. The only thing remotely close to this sensation was her memory as a teenager in a haunted house with fake spider webs grazing against her skin via a short kiddie train ride.

She crouched down, trying to squeeze in behind the cabinet. She tried not to breathe, tried not to think.

Helen realized something was missing. The world had gone deaf—void of sound.

Maybe they left. Maybe they gave up.

She took in a helpless gulp of air and held it.

Straining to listen, to hear anything now, her eyes felt so open, like her pupils had dilated to the size of pennies.

Nothingness.

She crouched down onto all fours in the slice between the wall and the cabinet, trying to get more comfortable. She heard the cat mew once and knew he was close but didn't know where. She reached her hands out, patting at the cool concrete floor, searching for him.

A streak of light blazed on. Someone had flipped on the light switch. It angled through the dark garage, spotlighting the opposite side of the room, by the entry for cars, by the tambour door.

Helen blinked. Her pupils shrunk immediately.

The glaring light cascaded around the bodies of the two men.

Helen huddled alone, motionless. Her arms covered her head. The gritty floor pressed hard against her forehead.

"Did you think you could hide?"

Lifting her head, she saw two sets of men's shoes. She began to cry.

"Did you think you could hide?" He repeated with more intensity, commanding her to speak.

"Don't do this."

"Don't do what, honey?" He stepped closer.

Tanner followed him. "Don't do what?"

"Look. I'll just go back to Seattle. I'll disappear. I'll never say a word." Her voice warbled out the words, begging.

"No. Now, you know that won't work for any of us." He shifted his eyes onto Tanner. "Get her. We need to take her somewhere else."

As Tanner approached her, Helen screamed. "Shut up, bitch." He cracked her across the cheek with a fist. Helen fell to the side and onto the floor at the base of the cabinet. She scrambled on her side away from him, but it proved useless. He was on her fast. Pulling her up to her feet with both hands—one hand gripping the back of her shirt and the other snagged within her hair. He steadied her and then punched her in the face again.

"Okay. That's enough. We don't want any blood in

here." Hawthorne walked over to both of them, grabbing one of Helen's arms and leading her in front of him. "Take her car. I'll take Helen."

****

The deadbolt didn't click over when she turned the key inside the side door lock. She didn't remember locking it, but she also didn't remember not locking it either. Habits she just took for granted sometimes. Although today, Georgette parked her car, her little white Suzuki Grand Vitara, in the driveway instead of inside the garage. It needed a wash; plus, this spring day looked too inviting to drive inside and walk through the garage, inside through the bathroom, and into the house. She wanted to stay outside as long as possible today.

"Gangster! Mommy's home." She repeated the same words each day upon returning from work. "Kitty, want some food?"

She set her purse and keys down on the kitchen counter and toed the heel of her left shoe, pulling it off, then did the same to her right.

"Gangster. Kitty." She untied her apron as she walked to the washer. Pulling it over her head, she tossed the soiled thing into the machine and closed the lid. "Gangster. Where are you, you little monster?"

He wasn't in his usual spot on the couch. "Gangster? Where are you?" She remembered closing the coat closet earlier and wondered if he might've gotten shut inside there, but then remembered petting him before she left. She checked the coat closet anyway, and to no surprise, he was not inside. She remembered him jumping up onto the kitchen counter. Then she questioned her memory. Was it yesterday or today?

Looking inside the open door of the bathroom, Georgette checked to see if he might be there, curled up on a towel. No sign there either. "Gangster!" She had a couple other places she could look before she needed to panic. Her mind flashed on the kitchen door being unlocked.

"Darn it, Gangster. When I find you..." Her voice trailed off from her fake threat.

Stopping in the hallway, she looked around with her hands on her waist. She turned to the left, then the right, wondering why she couldn't find her cat.

She walked to the couch again and looked at the spot where he normally slept. She felt it, checking to see if it was warm. But it was cool. She rubbed her hands now over the entire surface of the couch, worrying about where her cat was hiding. She bent down to her knees and laid her cheek against the floor, looking with one eye closed and the other targeted under the piece of furniture. He wasn't there either.

She raised up, knees bent, sitting next to the couch. "Gangster!" Her voice croaked out. "Kitty, honey. Where are you?" She felt her heart skip into a quicker pace but tried to calm down, to think of other hiding places, other options where she might search.

Finally, she rose and walked fast to the open door where Helen had stayed. The mustiness of the room had been replaced with something fouler, something dirty. It smelled of Helen's perfume and Hawthorne. Her nose twitched at the odor, but she went inside anyway and pulled the chain to the ceiling fan, sending it whirling for circulation. Then she opened up the window for the draft to wash the room clean. She checked under

Helen's bed.

He wasn't anywhere.

Nearly at a run now, leaving doors open, she raced through the living room and outside through the French doors, calling for her cat there.

After a half-hour, she decided to call Roberta. When she pressed the button, the distinct *beep-beep-beep* of a message still waiting on her voice mail buzzed in her ear. Messages left by Hawthorne. Messages left by Helen.

But then she wondered if maybe someone else had left a message about her cat.

She dialed her voice mail, pressed in her password, and listened.

Hawthorne's begging voice pissed her off immediately, and she deleted all four of his entreaties without listening all the way to the end.

Helen's messages disturbed her the most, making Georgette feel betrayed all over again.

"Georgette," her voice sounded urgent. Not what Georgette would have expected, so she listened further. "Georgette. Look. It's important you call me. I need your help. Oh. No..." A muffling through the mouthpiece, and then the phone went dead.

Georgette deleted it. Just like Helen. Weak, pitiful, deceitful, conniving, untrustworthy, no-good Helen.

It was Helen's second message she decided to keep. "Hello, Georgette. Don't worry about me. Like I said in my note, I've decided to go back to Seattle. I'm leaving Thursday morning on an early bus."

The complete reversal seemed odd. Her voice didn't sound the same. The urgency had been replaced by something different, something sounding like surrender.

She didn't say goodbye when the phone went dead.

This time she called Roberta, asking her to help find Gangster.

Georgette went to the cupboard and grabbed a can of cat food. She unzipped its lid—a final sure-fire way to get her cat to come to her—hoping the familiar sound, the ensuing call of "Zummy" would bring Gangster back.

Chapter 11

"Yes. Helen Wellen's room. I believe she's staying at your hotel. Thank you."

Music intermixed with hotel ads looped in Georgette's ear for so long she switched the phone to the other ear. The hotel operator came back on the line, saying no one was answering.

"Yes, please. A voice message will be fine. Thank you." Georgette agreed.

The robot recorder announced Helen as the guest and instructed Georgette to speak after the brief tone. A bell droned, and Georgette began.

"Helen, it's Georgette Carlisle. Look, I'm leaving Sunnydale for a while. I'm calling for two things—first, you're not getting any part of my diner. Roberta has decided to buy in, so looks like you're out. Don't even think about contacting a lawyer. I'll fight it until I have to sell the diner to some grifter if that's what it takes to keep you out. And second, you can have *all* of Hawthorne Biggs. Goodbye, Helen. I hope we never see each other again."

She hung up hard. She hoped the sound would be violent upon Helen listening to the message.

****

Nearly six hours passed, and Gangster still hadn't returned when Georgette finally went to bed at midnight. Her anxiety made her wake up during the night, rising every hour, looking around the house for him, going outside, calling his name, shining the flashlight, searching the desert around her house.

She wondered if her mind was playing tricks on her? She thought she heard him—that slight muffled mew of him calling in desperation. But the windy night sucked the sound away so fast it nearly laughed at her, letting her know how powerless she really was.

Giving up each time, she returned to bed feeling somehow Gangster knew she was searching for him but kept missing him. She couldn't help but feel she was letting him down. She refused to think the unthinkable.

Her eyes hung heavy with exhaustion when the doorbell chimed.

She climbed out of bed. It was late the following morning, and she still had to get to the diner. They could serve a leftover, call it the day's special, and serve it with extras for a dollar cheaper than yesterday's dinner.

The disappearance of her cat had consumed her now, as did the dismantling of her future with Hawthorne.

Peering through the spyhole in the door, Georgette saw Roberta looking around outside, waiting for her.

"Hey, Rob. I can't believe this," she said as she opened the door for her.

"When did you see him last?"

"Yesterday morning before work. I'm going nuts."

Roberta walked in and, seeing no coffee had yet been made, went over to the pot and helped herself. She cranked open the water, filled the glass pot, and poured it into the maker. Then she opened a cupboard and pulled out a can of coffee. Something she always kidded Georgette about, but today she didn't comment. Today Georgette wouldn't take kidding kindly.

"Well, maybe if you take one side of the property and I take the other, we might flush him out."

"I don't know, Rob. It's like, well, I've looked all over out there. He never goes off too far, and even if he did, it's not like we couldn't spot him a mile away. It's barren, just a couple of mesquite. It's not like he can hide."

"No. You're right. Gosh, George, what could've happened to him?" She paused and then spoke the thing Georgette had feared the most. "Do you think he got hit by a car?"

"Oh, Rob, please. I thought I left him inside yesterday. I don't remember, though. Everything's been so topsy-turvy in my life. Poor Gangster. It's not his fault."

"Well, don't worry yet."

"But, Rob. I neglected him because of Hawthorne, and now look what happened."

"Georgette, now listen. Did you feed him?"

She nodded fast.

"Give him water?"

Nodding again, she answered. "Yes, of course. He's like my own child. He's my family. I did everything to keep him alive, but I guess I must've forgotten about him needing me lately. I've been so wrapped up with everything about Hawthorne these days." Georgette's face tightened. Her jaw quivered under the stress of trying not to cry, but tears welled in her eyes anyway. "It's been over twenty-four hours, Roberta." She blurted out.

"Okay. Well, let's start searching. I mean, we can

talk about it all day long, but that won't help. I'll take the outside."

"All right. Thanks, Rob."

"I'm going to take a cup of that coffee there with me, though."

Georgette ignored Roberta's attempt at lightening the mood and walked back into her bedroom to change. The sheets on the bed lay in a mangled heap. Four pillows had been tossed helter-skelter, two up where she put her head and the others trailing toward the foot of the bed. She hadn't put her shoes away for a week. Her dresser had accumulated a mess of things from her pockets—her change, a tube of lipstick, notes from work, Helen's note, a wad of Kleenex, her car keys, and her engagement ring. Discarded things she should deal with—later. Later, when she had the energy. The mess lay about not only cluttering the room but also cluttering her mind to the point she allowed her anger for Helen to cloud her responsibility for Gangster, to the point she misplaced him. Was her cat also something she'd subconsciously discarded? She didn't want to consider being so irresponsible.

A sharp pain swelled in her throat. She swallowed what felt like a stone, a hot stone.

Finally, she resolved to make things right again, to turn her life around.

Her first priority? To find her cat.

At her dresser, she opened her underwear drawer, pulled out a pair of socks and a pair of panties, and tossed them onto the bed. She shimmied off her pajama bottoms, and sitting on the bed, she let them drop to the floor. She picked up her undies and slipped them on over her feet. She hadn't looked once at each article of clothing as she dressed but instead, she stared at the mess covering her dresser.

She lifted each sock and slipped them on—one foot at a time. Rising again, she shuffled back to the dresser, her eyes staying riveted to Helen's note. She pulled open her T-shirt drawer and looked in. She loved gray T-shirts; she guessed because she loved cloudy skies. She chose one reading, *I Survived 110° in Sunnydale,* and tossed it behind her onto the crumpled bed. She opened her jeans drawer and lifted out a pair of thin blue denims, shaking them once to loosen their creases, and, like the T-shirt, she flung them behind her over on the bed.

When she pulled off her thin floral nightshirt, it broke her stare from the items on her dresser, and she turned with the gown fully covering her face. Heading to the bed, she pulled her nightclothes completely off and dropped her arms, letting the shirt fall to the floor.

"Want some coffee, George?" Roberta yelled from the kitchen.

"I'll get it. Thanks, hon!" she screamed back.

She heard the front door close and knew Roberta had set off in search of Gangster.

"Oh my heavens, Gangster." The words groaned out of her. "Where are you, kitty?" She began to cry and sat on the bed to finish dressing. She could hear Roberta's muted calls for the cat outside.

Regaining composure, Georgette wiped her eyes with her fingers, but her nose began to run.

She slunk off the bed, reaching for her tissue, knocking Helen's note down in the process, and fell back into place on the edge of her bed, wiping her nose and looking at the piece of paper now lying on the floor.

"Crap." She didn't want to deal with it. Not yet.

Georgette aimed and threw the wadded tissue into the waste can by the dresser. It hit the edge and bounced off the rim.

"Crap, crap, crap." Now, she really had to get up, not only to pick up Helen's note but also to throw the tissue in the wastebasket. She passed the note to get the wadded tissue and tossed the wad in the garbage.

Then, looking at the note, she stepped over it, avoiding it still, and decided to make the bed first. It was a dance of sorts—Helen's note calling to Georgette and Georgette refusing the call. The excuse not to read it? A messy bed.

Pulling the sheets up tight, she fluffed the pillows into place and walked around the end of the bed. Ignoring Helen's note, she walked toward the headboard and pulled the sheets taut again on the other side, fluffing the pillows again and smoothing out the comforter.

She sat at the end of the bed again and stared at the note on the floor.

"Okay, Helen. What do you have to say this time?"

Finally, she bent over and picked up the crumpled note, found a corner, and unfolded it once, opening it up to its full size.

She began reading.

A trite apology came first, of course. Georgette rolled her eyes in disgust and read further. Helen had some things in the garage, in the empty cupboard. At the end of the note, she'd scribbled four numbers—*two, eight, one, four*. It must've been a piece of scrap paper she'd found and written on. Helen added she would pick everything up before leaving town, which would be tomorrow per her phone message.

Georgette decided she would leave a note for her on the kitchen door, telling Helen to help herself into the garage and to make sure she closed the garage door when she was done, to take her crap and just get the hell out. Things would finally be settled, and maybe she might start moving forward with her life again.

Georgette told herself she wouldn't answer her own door until she was sure Helen and her things were gone.

"Slut." She cursed under her breath and tossed the paper into the waste can, this time sinking the basket.

Then she looked under the bed, again, just in case—just in case he had been hiding for some reason, and she just hadn't noticed.

When she saw her cat wasn't there, Georgette retraced her steps again for what felt like the one-millionth time—into the bathroom, in linen closets, in the bathroom, inside the hall closets, searching Helen's room, reminding herself she had to quit thinking of it as Helen's room. Helen, who, by the way, had left the room in a disarray of paperwork, long legal-looking business papers. She was surprised she hadn't noticed them on Bobby's desk in the days before when she stripped the bed of its soiled sheets. She shuddered at the thought.

After bending down to view under the bed in Helen's room—again, she got up, looked inside the closet, in the guest bathroom, through the living room. Moving the coffee table away, she searched once more under the couch.

"Georgette." Roberta had come back inside, and

Georgette was once again on her knees at the base of the couch.

"Yeah. In here."

"Hey." Roberta appeared with two cups in her hands. "You have any yet?"

"No. Not yet. Thanks."

"Sure." She set Georgette's cup on the coffee table. Georgette stayed seated on the floor next to her cup.

"I looked everywhere outside but didn't find him."

Looking up at the window, Georgette noticed the clouds had filtered out the sun. "Son of a biscuit!" She picked up the cup and sipped without really tasting anything. "Wonder where he went." She shook her head as she sipped and then set the cup back on the table. Georgette pushed off the ground and reseated herself on the couch. Roberta sat down next to her.

"I have to get to the diner. Everybody will be showing up for work within an hour. I've gotten nothing done since yesterday."

"Look. Nothing's happening at my office." Roberta went on, "Don't know whatever kept Pyle so busy while he was mayor, but I'm so bored there I could…" Roberta took a gulp of her coffee and set her cup next to Georgette's. "Look, I can go into the diner. You get there as soon as you can, but I know what to do for lunch."

"Oh, would you, Rob? I'll pay you back. I promise."

"Yeah? Will you be the mayor for a day? Please?" She smiled at her friend. "Of course I can handle lunch. Just make sure you're there to prep for dinner."

Georgette nodded her head. "Thanks, hon. I owe you big time."

"Well, I suppose I should learn the dinner part too."

"It's not so hard. I'll teach you everything. Thanks for covering for me, Rob. I just need to do a couple of things around here, and I'll be there for dinner."

She stood at the door outside the kitchen next to the garage in the thermal warmth the coming storm had created and watched as Roberta drove off. She thought she heard Gangster's familiar yowl, but he was nowhere in sight. She blamed the wind again. She looked around, waving Roberta off, and then placed one hand to her mouth. She decided to open the garage now. Helen might come by today if she was leaving early tomorrow. But first, she went back into the kitchen to grab a pen and piece of paper. She scratched out a terse note letting Helen know to help herself into the garage, the cabinet, and to remember to shut the door when she was finished. She didn't even sign her name.

She found the tape dispenser in a drawer and stuck the note to the door, walked to the car she'd left parked in the driveway, reached inside the driver's window, and pressed the garage opener sitting on the console. The garage door jostled and creaked so Georgette didn't hear Gangster's yowl upon him hearing the door opening.

Instead, she hung there, her head and shoulders inside the cab, and watched to make sure it didn't come down again automatically as it sometimes did. This time it didn't. The garage gaped open, and the tambour door stayed up. She went back inside the house and headed off down the hallway to her bedroom, to the bathroom inside her bedroom, and in the master bathroom to take a long, hot shower.

Chapter 12

"Georgette. You're being a damn stubborn woman."

"Look, Hawthorne. We can't talk now. I have a full dinner crowd. I don't have time for…" she waved her arms as if searching for a word, "this." His eyes followed her hand as she gestured.

"We need to talk."

"Not now, Hawthorne." She pressed out his name, opening her eyes wide for emphasis. "I can't."

"When, then?"

Georgette turned back to a customer's plate she was dressing. She delicately placed five sprigs of asparagus next to a filet of salmon and poured a lemon cream sauce over the fish.

"Tomorrow!" she barked. "We can talk tomorrow." She turned quickly, however, from the plate and added, "Call first. And don't you dare just show up or come to my house."

"Fine." His eyes flashed silver in anger. "Fine. I'll call you tomorrow at nine."

"Fine." She snarled back, glaring at him and continuing to stare until he left her kitchen. He walked toward the back door, and she followed. He opened it and stepped through. She grabbed it and began to close it. He turned around as if to say something else. She looked him squarely in the eyes and closed the door

Susan Wingate

without letting him speak.

"He gone?" Roberta asked as she came into the kitchen.

"Yes. The salmon dish is there. Sorry. I was seeing Hawthorne out."

"Did you two talk?"

"How can we? Look how busy it is." She walked over to the plate and handed it to Roberta. "He's calling tomorrow." She rolled her eyes and shook her head. "Can you make the salad?"

"Yep." Roberta grabbed a salad plate and began dishing organic greens onto it, placing grape and cherry tomatoes in a pile in the center and adding three slivers of hearts of palm, then finishing it off by drizzling their sweet signature balsamic dressing over the top. She picked up both plates and looked at Georgette with a smile across her plump, red lips. She always looked so pretty to Georgette when she played hostess for the dinner crowd.

"I need to pee." Georgette really just needed to sit and relax alone in the bathroom, to be alone, if only for a second. She patted down several unruly hairs on the side of her head and wiped her hands on her white chef jacket. "I should wear my hat."

Roberta continued to smile and walked through the swinging doors, taking the food to their patrons.

Five minutes later, Georgette came out of the bathroom. It was only eight o'clock. They still had another solid thirty minutes until people began thinning out. Cammy was in the kitchen, rustling through her purse for her pack of cigarettes.

"Make it quick." Georgette hated hiring smokers, but Cammy had been one of the most reliable, hardest-working gals they had. She could smoke, wash her hands, rinse her mouth out, and be back out on the floor within five minutes. Georgette paid her well for it, too. Cammy had a kid, a small house she was trying to buy, and a dog, the newest addition to her small family. She'd gotten it for her boy. She wanted to teach him how to be responsible—for himself and for another living thing—something Georgette obviously couldn't yet accomplish at middle age. She felt so guilty about losing Gangster. She agonized between worrying about her cat and dealing with Hawthorne.

By nine, she had peeled off her chef coat and started putting the kitchen back in order. She needed to go home to see if Gangster had returned. To see if Helen had been by.

By nine-thirty, she asked Roberta to lock up. She happily agreed.

By nine forty-five, she was driving her car up to her house. The lights angled across the driveway, glaring into the open mouth of the garage. Helen had yet to come by. The headlights spread over the front yard, reflecting off the windows and slanting down the street, fading off in the distance and giving the evening an eerie glow.

She parked on the street. If Helen needed to put her things in her car, she wanted the driveway clear for her.

The engine hummed and died when she turned the key off. Opening the car door, the smell of the desert night struck her first. Creosote cooling under the stars giving off its spicy tar scent seemed to be as fragrant as when it warmed under the day's sun.

The stars blanketed the black sky, and Georgette spotted the Big Dipper. Following it up and finding the

North Star, she located the Little Dipper next to it, sort of upside-down, and breaking the peaceful night, she yelled out, "Gangster!" Then adding in a high note, she yelled the universal call for all cats, "Kitty, kitty, kitty!" She paused, bending her ear to the evening ground, and called again, "Kitty! Gangster!"

Giving up, she wondered how many times she would go out tonight calling for him. She listened at her front door. Heard the distant barking of coyotes in the prairie and dreaded her cat's possible fate.

****

She'd slept until the breaking sun shone against a wall and lit up the living room. Georgette remembered going outside only a few times last night to look for Gangster. Exhaustion sent her to sleep on the couch, watching an old rerun of Law & Order during one of their usual marathons. Another episode was playing on the TV with the volume so low when her eyes opened, she thought the sound was a fly buzzing around.

She reached for the remote and clicked it off.

Stepping into her slippers and shuffling toward the kitchen, she yawned while emptying yesterday's cold coffee from the pot and running water to rinse it clean. As she stood refilling the pot, she looked over at the clock above the kitchen table. Six-thirty. After pouring the water into the coffee maker and starting it, making sure it began to drip, she walked to the front door and looked through a window. She remembered leaving her car on the street and why, but she hadn't heard anyone drive to her house. Instead, she knew she had slept soundly.

Unlocking the door and opening it, a blast of cool desert air streamed into Georgette's face. She smelled the muddy adobe earth mixed with a strong whiff of the jasmine vining along the side of her driveway. The delicate, star-shaped flowers intoxicated a few bees who alighted languidly as they collected powdery, mustard-colored pollen along their legs and underbellies.

But the cool, heavy air made her skin prickle, and she wrapped her arms around her.

Before going back inside, she noticed the garage door was still up. Georgette realized Helen could have come, cleaned out whatever was in there of hers, and left without closing the garage—no matter how insistent Georgette had been about closing it.

Instantly, her face went hot with anger. "Stupid cow."

She slammed the kitchen door and once again thought she heard the muffled sound of a cat's mew. "Gangster!" she said as she swung the door open fast. Not wanting to give up on the search, she thought she heard him again. She closed the door behind her.

The sound pulled her closer to the garage.

She looked around. After yelling his name, everything seemed to go deaf again; even birds and bees seemed to halt.

Turning one way, then the other, she remembered she had never once looked inside the garage. But why would she? He couldn't have possibly gotten into the garage without someone letting him in. "Gangster," she repeated.

Once again, nothing. The mewing stopped when she called him.

In an instant, she realized how it had been for the last two nights. Whenever she heard him crying, she would call his name, making him think she was coming for him, which made him stop calling to her.

Just inside the door of the garage, she froze. She barely took in air. Looking from one side of the garage to the other, she remained quiet. The place was sparse except for a worktable, the garbage, recycling cans, and a set of storage cabinets marked *BD-Files* where Bobby had stored old diner information. There was a combination lock through the hasp, which locked the double doors. The lock was new. The lock hadn't been there before. It was the only thing out of place. Her eyes latched onto the cabinet. "Oh no! Gangster."

She heard a shred of noise from the direction of the cabinet and ran over. "Gangster?"

He cried. It was him. She'd heard him distinctly, his mewling, a meow loud enough to break Georgette's heart.

"Oh, my Lord! Gangster! How did you...?" She trailed off as she examined the lock. She didn't know the combination.

But, wait.

She did know the combination.

The four numbers on Helen's note. They meant something! She had to find her note. Running off, yelling behind her, she called out, "Gangster. I'll be back, honey!"

Nearly slipping on the Saltillo kitchen tile, she hung onto the door for only a moment when she ran into the house. Then she ran down the hall and into her bedroom. To the waste bucket. To the note.

She uncrumpled the wad of paper. *Two, eight, one, four.*

She ran back through the hall, through the kitchen,

out the door, and back into the garage "Gangster!" The cat mewed inside the cupboard. "I'm here, honey." Through her panicked breathing, she repeated, "I'm here." It had been nearly three days he'd been locked inside the cabinet. Her hands shook as she held the lock in them. She stared down at its black face trimmed in a neat circle of white numbers, spaced in increments of five, beginning with the number zero and ending at thirty-nine.

She tried twenty-eight first, then one, then four. The lock remained tight. But maybe it was because her hands were shaking terribly. She tried the combination again. Twenty-eight, one, four. Nothing.

She paused and breathed in, then out. Then she stopped and took one deep breath and let it out slowly.

Georgette examined the lock again and knew the only plausible next set of numbers. Two, eight, and fourteen.

She turned to the right to two, and then, slowly passing by the eight, she landed there on the next pass. She paused and took in a deep breath again. Gangster let out a low groan. "Okay, honey. I'm here. Just hold on a little longer, baby." She turned the dial slowly, slowly enough to know she hadn't made a mistake. She stopped. Then she pulled hard, once. The lock unlatched.

Fumbling with the thing through the hasp's looping metal felt grueling. She finally got it off and pulled the door open wide.

Gangster stumbled out. Yowling, objecting, he sat down only a foot outside of his jail. He was gaunt and visibly weakened. He needed water. He needed a can of cat food.

A waft of foul air struck her. The odor from the cabinet stung her eyes. It had been his bed and cat box for three days.

Georgette dropped the lock onto the concrete floor, startling the cat. Then she scooped him up into her arms, holding him tighter than she probably should have and cooing to him how she missed him.

She sped back into the house. He needed rehydration and food.

Chapter 13

Georgette stood embarrassed in front of the jeweler. Sunnydale was a small town. She was sure everyone already knew about her and Hawthorne, how their relationship fell to pieces before getting started. She tried to shoo the thoughts out of her head, concentrating instead on the fact she'd found her lost cat.

"Oh, now, let me see that gorgeous thing." Paul Kessler examined the ring through his eyeglass and paused.

"Can you give me an idea of how much I might get for it, Paul?" Georgette's eyes looked puffy and owlish from the makeup she had applied, trying to hide the fact she'd been crying.

Paul had owned Sunnydale's finest jewelry store since before computers came into fashion. Georgette often thought he looked an awful lot like Mark Twain with his wild white hair and mustache. The band around his head with a single magnifying glass for viewing jewels seemed almost for show, since he used his loupe instead. He flipped each layered lens of the loupe out in succession, squeezing one eye tight for a better view. Then, in quick succession, he closed each layer again— one, two, three. He rose up straight when he finished the inspection of Georgette's engagement ring, the one Hawthorne had given her.

It had been a difficult decision to redeem the ring for cash. It felt cheap, but then she thought about how she might use the money—for employee bonuses, for new linens for the tables.

She tussled between giving the ring back, which meant having to see Hawthorne, or cashing it in. She decided cashing it in seemed right.

Yet, still, as she stood in the jewelry store, she vacillated. She cursed herself, thinking she'd already decided. But maybe not, not really, as it turned out after all.

There, she was not sure again if cashing in the ring was the right decision. Maybe it wasn't. Maybe it was too soon. She didn't want to keep his ring or anything else to remind her of him in the house. She certainly didn't want to ever meet up with him again, to see him face-to-face and give the thing back. She supposed she could mail it to him. She didn't know what to do, not really. And, just as she was thinking of how she might mail it, of all the possibilities, Paul spoke.

"Georgette." He extended the last syllable of her name far too long.

"Oh. Yes?" Jolted, she looked at him, surprised. "This here pretty little ring is, um, I'm afraid to say, not worth very much."

"What?"

"This here stone," he didn't even say gem, "is what we call a cubic zirconium." He handed the ring back to her. She took it almost involuntarily, staring at it the whole time.

"But he said it was worth…" She closed her eyes, realizing Hawthorne had played her again. She tried to regain some sense of decorum, her embarrassment flushing red over her face. "Oh, my goodness. Thank you, Paul." A fake smile, one she assumed to match the ring, cracked the corners of her mouth. "Well, this is quite a shock. I'm so sorry to have wasted your time." She wondered if the freckles over her cheeks had disappeared in the hot red mask she felt covering her face. "How embarrassing." Her hand came up to cover her mouth.

"Not at all, Georgette." He stood at the glass counter with both hands sitting on top of it. He had seen plenty of this, she guessed, over the years. "It's a beautiful setting, probably worth a good five hundred in metal. If you'd like, I can give it to you. Like I said, it's a beautiful setting."

And it was so simple. The decision. Giving it back or keeping it.

"That would be wonderful, Paul. Thank you. He said it was worth…" Why bother finishing her sentence when it didn't warrant repeating?

Paul sidestepped over to the cash register a foot or so from where they stood and pressed one key; the machine dinged, and he counted out five one-hundred-dollar bills. Pressure had built into her cheeks, and it was beginning to consume her nose and threatening to spread into her eyes like a match on alcohol. She felt an urge to cry come up so quickly she needed to repeat in her head, *don't cry* five times in quick succession. She pressed her fingers into her eye sockets and focused on her breathing, trying to assuage the potential onslaught of tears building.

Paul glanced from her to the register, then walked nearer to her, waving the money in his hand.

"Here you go," he said.

Georgette wondered if he could tell she was going to crumble at any moment.

As he counted the money into her hand, he added, "Let me just write you up a receipt, and you can be on your way." He bent down, taking his eyes off her for a second to pull out a packet of receipts. He wrote the appropriate information down, giving her time to collect herself.

He pulled off the carbon copy and handed it to her with a smile widening over his set of tea-stained teeth.

"Thanks, Paul."

"My pleasure. It's always a pleasure doing business with you, Georgette, always. Come back anytime."

"Thanks, Paul," she repeated, not able to get anything else out. To do so would be to cry. She folded the receipt into the stack of bills and pressed the whole thing into her jeans pocket. When she looked up, she gave Paul another short smile.

****

"I don't know, Roberta. I didn't go in there. I haven't been in the garage for days." Georgette fiddled with the cushion on the chair in front of Roberta's desk. The city hall buzzed today with people walking up and down the corridors. It felt like all of Sunnydale had shown up. Someone barked out the word, "Now!" down a few offices from what Georgette could determine. Roberta got up, closed the door, and then went back around her desk and sat.

They both paused after the interruption. "Well, um, how do you think he got...?"

"Like I said, I don't know." She bit her thumbnail. "You know, Roberta..."

"Mayor?" Roberta's administrative assistant called through the phone's intercom. "Phone call, line one, for you."

"Kelly, can you take a message? I'm right in the middle of something."

Roberta stared into Georgette's eyes as she spoke and mouthed "*Sorry*" to her after she finished speaking.

"Mayor, it's the police department. Said it's kind of urgent."

"Okay, Kelly. Will you tell them to hold for just one second? I'll be right with them."

"Yes, ma'am." The call beeped through. "Sorry, George, but I better take this."

"Should I wait, or should I leave?"

"No, please wait. It shouldn't take long."

When Roberta picked up the call and began to talk, Georgette realized how long it had been since she'd been in her office. The building had been erected in the early 1930s and still had the original red brick walls inside and out, but the interior brick had been painted with several layers of white, light green, or blue, depending on the year and the color du jour. The latest color gleamed a glossy milk-colored paint and, depending on where you sat in the room, looked either eggy or chalky in color. The room stunk of brand-new, commercial-grade, glued-down carpeting. The synthetic smell did battle with the scent of Roberta's favorite perfume, *Beautiful* by Estee Lauder.

From inside Roberta's office with the door closed, Georgette noted a muted thrumming. Outside, the day was churning up a mix of storm clouds. As Georgette looked around at the fake leather seats on rolled wooden chairs, Roberta's conversation took on a more serious tone, which took Georgette's mind off the updated, contemporary look of her office.

"But, because there was no ID on the body, you're not sure, are you, Willard? Yes, I'll let her know. She's right here. Yeah, call you back."

Georgette's brow wrinkled, and she tipped her head at Roberta. "What's going on?"

"Crap. Georgette." She shook her head, delaying what she needed to say, what she needed to tell her. "It's not good, George."

"Yeah."

"The police got a call this morning—" Roberta paused, then added, "from the Extended Stay Lodge."

Georgette cocked her head, frowning, not understanding. "Okay," her voice drifted off to spur Roberta to finish explaining.

"It was a homicide call, George."

"What? A homicide? In Sunnydale?" Georgette's face seemed to pucker all at once when she asked.

Roberta's face looked white, almost expressionless. If Georgette hadn't detected the terror in her eyes, she might not have made the connection. Roberta's gaze drifted to her desk, directed at nothing in particular, trying to find something, anything, then bounced back up, her eyes reconnecting with Georgette. Finally, Georgette got an inkling of what she might be alluding to.

"Wait." She paused. "No." She paused again. "Oh, man, Roberta. Why are you telling me this?"

"You need to come with me, George. We need to go right now."

"To the lodge? No. Why?"

Her inflection swung her words into a high pitch.

She couldn't believe she had to go to a crime scene.

"We have to make the identification."

"Oh, heavens, Roberta. No. I don't think you need me to…" Georgette pushed against the back of the chair like a wild, cornered animal, shaking her head.

"We have to, George." Roberta stood collecting her purse and her attaché. She pulled her suit jacket off the back of her chair and swung it around her shoulders, putting each arm through a sleeve. "We have to go. Now."

A dull silence lay between them. Roberta stood strong in front of Georgette, who remained seated.

Then, as if avoiding the question might protect her, she finally spoke. "Identify whom?"

Roberta picked up both her bags in one hand, then picked up Georgette's and handed it to her. She grabbed Georgette by the arm, lifting her off the chair in the same movement. Roberta pulled Georgette close, held her around the shoulder, and led her out of the office. Then, as she flicked off the light and pulled the door closed, she simply said, "Helen."

Chapter 14

The drive was only five minutes from Roberta's office, but their silence made it feel like hours. As the car approached the hotel parking lot, Georgette saw the sun had dropped to the other side of noon, away from the coming storm. Shadows fell long on the side of the hotel where what seemed like a mile of yellow crime scene tape was strung.

Roberta parked about one hundred paces from the first police car—intended to block nosy people from entering. Every local knew every other local in Sunnydale, and they needed to keep the interlopers of their small town out. Still, the law was more lenient for a local than for someone who might be passing through. Which is why authorities wouldn't flinch if they saw Georgette approaching to identify Helen's body. People knew Georgette was one of Helen's closest relations since Mayor Pyle died.

After turning the engine off, she flicked open the locks on her attaché and pulled out a badge designating her official purpose for being there. Pinning it to her lapel, she instructed Georgette, "Okay. Look. This is going to be awful. There's no way of saying it nicer than that." Georgette didn't expect less from Roberta, who continued, "They will unzip the bag. You look once. Then, you turn your head as soon as you see the face. Hear me?"

Georgette stared blankly into her eyes. "Georgette. You hear me?"

She nodded. "Okay."

"So, tell me what you're going to do."

"Oh my, Roberta."

"Tell me, George. If anything needs to be practiced, this does. Tell me."

"They'll unzip the bag. I'll look once." When Georgette said *once*, Roberta held one finger up, pressing it at her. "And as soon as I see the face, I'll turn my head away."

"Good." They looked at each other.

"Once." Roberta's face seemed unusually calm to Georgette, who couldn't seem to get her eyes to blink.

"Maybe it's not her."

Roberta sat back in her seat. Then she grabbed the door handle and pulled. "Maybe."

She looked back at Georgette, but Roberta's face made Georgette know instantly the body could belong to no one other than Helen. She started to cry. "I can't."

"You have to. I can't. I'm involved since the police work for the mayor. They need someone independent of the office." She stood outside with the door open. "You have to quit crying."

Georgette pushed open the heavy door and stepped in line after Roberta. She wiped her nose on her sleeve. "I'm sorry." She was the unofficial party here, yet everyone knew her.

Willard saw Roberta's car and walked past the first police car in a half-trot. "Mayor." He nodded to Roberta, then turned his attention to Georgette, "Mrs. Carlisle."

She'd forgotten how formal people were in

Susan Wingate

circumstances like this.

"Willard." When she said his name, he frowned.

Roberta turned quickly. "It's Police Chief, George."

"Oh, Willy. I'm sorry, Willard, uh, Police Chief. I'm so sorry."

"It's okay, Mrs. Carlisle. This way, ladies." He led them closer to the body, letting them follow him. "Try not to walk outside of where I'm stepping," he called back, making Georgette look down as she walked. Lights flashed. No one was speaking, not by the time they reached the ambulance anyway. Any talk had hushed when they recognized the person being brought in to identify the body.

A black bag lay upon a portable gurney. It seemed like there should be a siren blaring or a dirge, people praying…anything, but the only thing Georgette heard was a soft breeze hitting the yellow tape as it flapped, as it snapped to and fro in the wind. The lack of noise sent a shiver starting on Georgette's skull, cloaking her skin like a hat and snaking down across her shoulders.

Finally, Willard spoke. "Georgette, will you be okay?"

Her voice stalled, and she wondered why he asked—if she was going pale, if she looked like she might faint—but when she did answer, her voice nearly disappeared into her throat. "Yes, sir…" She coughed to clear her throat, "I'm okay."

He gestured for her to step in closer, past Roberta, and to stand next to him by the gurney.

Georgette looked back at Roberta, who tipped her head at the black bag, signaled to her with a single finger, and mouthed the word "*once*" as she gestured.

Then Roberta pulled her finger down and placed the nail of it into her mouth. She was clearly rattled.

"Mrs. Carlisle?" Willard's words barely registered in Georgette's mind, and he repeated, "Mrs. Carlisle? We're going to lift the plastic now. Are you ready?" He looked at Georgette and then over to Roberta. She could see Roberta nodding from her peripheral vision. As he reached to pull up the plastic, Georgette placed her hand on his arm, stopping him. She placed the other hand on her chest and took in a few deep breaths.

"Oh, my." The air escaped when she spoke. "Oh, this is terrible. Let me breathe. I need to catch my breath." She held his arm down and took in two more deep breaths. Then she slowly slid her hand off his arm and placed it near her eyes, ready to cover them if she had to.

When he rolled the plastic off, Georgette said to herself, *only once.* She would look only once like Roberta had told her.

But the problem was, she couldn't stop looking. No, not looking—staring. Georgette's eyes felt glued to Helen's face. She couldn't stop staring at her or the sheets. They looked so familiar. As she stared, she thought, *Weren't those the same ones off the guest bed? The ones she'd given to Hawthorne to dispose of?*

As she stared, she noticed how Helen's face didn't look normal. It was the face of someone older now, someone sad—old and sad. Not what she expected. But it was Helen, just not the Helen she remembered.

With her eyes, Georgette traced a thin streak of blood along her hairline, blood dripping from her right eye. Her nose was caved in—the blow must have killed her. She saw bruising had already begun to appear on her forehead, and rings shadowed her eyes like a raccoon, but these rings didn't look black. They looked blue. Georgette heard people talking behind her, voices rising like someone switched a loud radio on, but the words jumbled like everyone talking at the same time. The words were directed at her. Then someone's hand grabbed her shoulder and pulled her back.

She still couldn't take her eyes off Helen.

Willard covered Georgette's view by blocking her with his body.

The next thing she knew, Georgette had her face buried in Roberta's shoulder.

She heard her voice quaver through tears as she answered Willard when he asked if she knew the deceased.

"It's Helen," she said.

Then she was walking back to Roberta's car. "I only looked once."

When the car engine started up, she said it again, "I only looked once."

The car shimmied forward, felt as though it were on a conveyor belt. Then suddenly they were back home.

After they got out, Roberta held her around the shoulders as they walked to the door. Roberta had somehow fished her house key out and was opening the door for her. They walked together inside, where Gangster lay waiting for her on the kitchen counter. Roberta closed the door and helped Georgette to the kitchen table.

****

Roberta was going on and on about how she was only supposed to look once—a short once—as she hustled about the kitchen, getting water, going through cupboards, futzing. The words slid off Georgette because the past was gone, and now she was thinking about the present and what lay ahead. And what lay ahead didn't look rosy at all.

She interrupted Roberta's tirade, "Those were my sheets."

"What?"

"Helen. The sheets."

"Yeah?"

"They were mine."

Roberta unscrewed the bottle of scotch she had located and poured it into two glasses. "I'll see you get them back."

"No. I don't care about that. That's not what I mean."

Roberta turned to her, holding both glasses in between three fingers. She reached into the freezer, pulled some ice out of the bin, dropped some in each glass, and closed the freezer door again. "What do you mean, then?"

"I don't want the sheets back. I took them off the bed. After...you know." She toggled her head and grimaced.

"Okay. So?"

"So, then I put them in a plastic bag and took them to the diner. I meant to incinerate them. But then Hawthorne showed up."

Roberta took another sip and sat down across from Georgette at the table. "And..."

"Roberta, for crying out loud." Her eyes shot back and forth from one of Roberta's eyes to the other. "Don't you get it?"

"Guess not. Get what?"

"I gave those sheets to Hawthorne." She opened her eyes wide, hoping it would illuminate something in Roberta.

Roberta set her drink down very slowly, not looking at it but finding the table anyway. "Oh, dear Lord. You're not thinking—"

"We have to tell Willard, Rob. Those sheets went from my hand to Hawthorne. How did they end up wrapped around Helen?"

Georgette looked at her drink once, lifted it, and slugged it back in three gulps. By the time she finished and set the glass back on the table, Roberta had her cell phone out, dialed, and up to her ear.

Looking around the room, she felt scared somehow. She went over to get the cat, who had fallen asleep on the counter. Leaving him there in his solitude, she picked up the receiver on her phone. The distinct *beep beep beep* of a voice message rang in her ear. She dialed the number to retrieve the missed messages. There was only one—from Hawthorne.

Anger fumed through his words. She hadn't taken his call. Did she know whom she was dealing with? How could she? He was trying to patch things up, and she was being a bitch. He mentioned the ring, something like, *"You can keep the ring,"* laughing, but with anger spewing through the phone. She hung up, making sure not to press the delete button on the keypad.

Roberta, still speaking to Willard, didn't catch the fear in her face. Georgette opened the scotch bottle again and poured two more drinks, waiting for Roberta's call to end.

Staring at the floor, Georgette watched as Roberta flipped her phone closed. Roberta's face had gone through a gamut of emotions in the last couple of days, ranging from worry about her to scorn about Helen, to sadness, to fear and anger, and something else Georgette couldn't identify—a look like something between horror and fury.

"What." It wasn't a question.

"The coroner has made a preliminary examination of her body."

"Homicide, right?"

"Yes." She twitched her head up and down and grabbed her second drink, slugging half of it back and then setting it down, staring at it the whole time. A new look had brushed over her eyes, a sensitive, compassionate look. Roberta's eyes watered. She put both hands over her face.

"Rob. What?"

"Oh, George, there seems to have been a molestation as well."

"A molestation? What does that mean?" Helen had been beaten and tossed about. What more of a molestation could there be?

"A sexual molestation." Roberta pinned Georgette's eyes with hers.

"Oh, my Lord. No. No, no." Georgette's hand covered her mouth as she repeated the words until they sounded like an elegy, a psalm.

"During the preliminary, they noticed vaginal tearing and bruising."

"They did that there?" Georgette pushed her drink back away from her. She stood, looking nowhere in particular and toward the kitchen. Then she looked at

Roberta. "You don't think…"

Roberta looked at her with pity.

"No, Rob. That couldn't have been Hawthorne." She crossed both hands over her heart. "No. Not Hawthorne, Roberta. He wouldn't do anything like that. Would he? I mean, he was never rough or anything with me. You know? Always a gentleman, Rob. Oh, sure, we'd play, and he'd slap my butt every now and…No, Rob. It wasn't Hawthorne. Was it?"

"You really shouldn't be telling me anything more, George."

In lieu of the new information, Georgette seemed tenser. But how could he? There was no way in hell Hawthorne had been a party to any of this. She had to somehow let Willard know.

"It wasn't Hawthorne, Rob. We need to let the police know."

"They have evidence, Georgette."

"What kind of evidence?" Her face darkened again, and her eyes welled with tears.

"Well, the sheet, Georgie. Crap. They have the sheet. You said yourself…"

"It could've been stolen from his truck. He might've just tossed it in a garbage can somewhere, and some homicidal maniac fished it out. He's not like that, Roberta. He's not a murderer, and he's certainly not a rapist."

Roberta saw how riled Georgette was becoming and tried to appease her by saying, "Well, we just have to let the police do their job now. It's out of our hands."

But Georgette stuck to the subject like a fox chasing a rabbit, "You have to tell them that Hawthorne has never even shown an inkling of being like, like, like that! Roberta. Please! Call them back."

****

Sunshine cracked through the whitewashed shutters of the lawyer's office. The room—decorated meagerly, some would call it contemporary, with desert motifs and lithographs of saguaro and roadrunners on the jade walls—felt organized. The floor contrasted warmly with a powdery washing of pinkish pine planks. Georgette and Roberta sat side by side in front of his desk in run-of-the-mill metal office chairs with comfortable tweed upholstered seats and rounded wooden armrests.

Kaplan Hayes had been the same lawyer who had read Bobby's will five years before to three of Bobby's women—Georgette, Roberta, and Vanessa, Roberta's mom. It made for an uncomfortable couple of minutes as they got reacquainted until, of course, Hayes spoke and asked them to sit.

"Now, why didn't we do this all five years ago and just cut to the chase?" The wide smile on his thick face had nothing but kindness behind it, and his words broke the ice. When he laughed, his neck jiggled around his collar, making the tie look like a noose around a hanging man.

Smiling lately was difficult in light of all the information implicating Hawthorne in Helen's lust murder. As Roberta kept referring to her death. But she smiled at Georgette, trying to show a sense of camaraderie between them for the lawyer. Georgette reached out to Roberta and grabbed her hand.

"We're slow learners, aren't we, Rob?"

"Guess so."

Roberta appeared nervous to Georgette, almost to

111

the same level of nervousness as the day they went to the hotel.

"Mr. Hayes—"

He interrupted. "Call me Kaplan, Georgette, please."

"Kaplan. Thank you. Kaplan, we wanted to know how long all this will take." Roberta had to review the police report on Helen; all of a sudden, her office was popping in activity because of Helen's murder.

"Basically, you sign, and you sign," he tipped his head toward Roberta. "We have an office witness—one of the gals in here can do that—notarize it, and it's a done deal. The technical stuff, like filing and making copies, we do all that for you. That's why you pay me the big bucks, Georgette." He flashed another fat smile at her. "Once you sign these here papers, the deal has been brokered. Of course, either one of you has the boilerplate seventy-two hours to renege. If you don't, basically, it's a done deal."

"Well, how about you get our witness in here, Kaplan. I'm ready. Are you, Rob?"

Roberta's head bounced fast. She hardly blinked as she stared at the document lying on the desk. Georgette was right. She was nervous.

So she patted Roberta's hand. "You want a glass of water or something, Rob? It looks like you're about to keel over."

Roberta turned to Georgette and flashed an awkward smile. "Are you sure about this, George? I mean, you don't have to do this, you know."

"I wouldn't want anything but this, Roberta. What if something were to happen to me? Who would get this place? Gangster?"

Roberta shrugged her shoulders, and Georgette continued, "That's right, no one, that's who. This way," her voice pitched up, "the diner stays in the family." Georgette paused and then nodded to Hayes to go get a witness. He rose and left the two women alone momentarily.

"I have to tell you, Roberta, I couldn't believe you refused to take your half of the diner after your mother died. She only left it to me because you had been so stub...so adamant about it."

"Honestly, George? I needed some time to deal with her death. I just would've been a one-hundred-and-sixty-pound piece of meat standing in your way. I just needed some time, that's all. I'd already resolved myself to the fact that if the chance came up again, I would agree."

"Oh, honey. I'm so glad to hear that." She patted her arm again and then crossed them both in her lap. "So why the nerves?"

"Holy crap, George. It's worth three point five million dollars!" she screamed, although attempting to hush her words. "I've never owned anything worth that much before."

"It's just money, Roberta. It's not God. It's how we pay our bills. It's how we pay our employees. It's a tool, not a status symbol. If you remember that, you'll be fine. Hell, you already know how to run the place."

Upon ending her statement, Kaplan Hayes walked back in with a tight-looking, thin-lipped woman who couldn't have been more than twenty-six, but her serious demeanor made her look much older.

"This is Candace Smally." She nodded at both women, said hello, and reached out to shake their hands.

"If you ladies will sign on the pages with the yellow sticky notes and initial every single page in this document, Candace will witness it for you." He yelled back over his shoulder, "Anytime, Beth. We don't want to go into the next ice age waiting for you." He winked at Georgette.

From down the hall, they could hear Hayes's wife responding, "I'm coming, Kaplan. Sorry." As the words grew closer, she entered the room. "I'm sorry, ladies…George, Roberta. I had to get off that blasted phone. I'm afraid it never stops ringing."

"Beth here will…"

"Hi, girls," Beth said again, smiling and acknowledging both women.

Hayes went on, "Beth'll notarize everyone's signature."

Roberta spoke low and nodded to Georgette, "You go first."

"Chicken." She chuckled and picked up one of the pens lying next to the contract.

"Shut up," Roberta chided back but smiled and picked up the other pen.

"You will owe me one thing, though." Georgette flipped sheets as she spoke, initialing and signing where indicated.

"What's that?" Roberta signed and initialed too. "If anything does happen to me, you have to promise to take care of Gangster."

Roberta chuckled, "I will. Did you even have to worry?"

Georgette grinned as she continued to initial the pages of the document as she got lost in thoughts of how this is what family did, they lived near each other, and they made something great together.

Chapter 15

Willard Cleary had been appointed to police chief a couple years back after he'd done such bang-up detective work discovering the killer of former Sunnydale mayor, Harold Pyle. He carried himself taller somehow. When he walked into the meeting room, Georgette felt the urge to stand and pushed her chair back to do so.

"Sit, please, Mrs. Carlisle." Hearing him refer to her by her proper name reminded Georgette Willy intended the meeting to be formal. He fingered the pencil he had stuck above his ear before closing the door and turning to her.

"Oh, thank you," she paused, wondering how she should address him again, and feeling Police Chief was too awkward to get out, she said, "Your Honor."

He looked at her as he pulled a chair from under the table to sit. A glint in his eyes showed her he thought the comment was funny.

"Crap, Willard, right. Sorry, Willy. I just should have stayed with Police Chief, right?"

"Georgette. Relax. Call me Willard for now. This is preliminary. If anyone else needs to be in the room with us, then call me Police Chief."

"Willy. Okay. Great. Thanks."

Her green eyes flashed at him. He squinted, smiling back at her.

"Your freckles match the color of your hair."

Georgette didn't know how to respond. She tugged at her ponytail and ground her rump down into the hardwood seat of the chair, then she wiped her hands across her face from the bridge of her nose to the edge of her cheeks. "Well," is all she managed to get out as she shook her head nervously and paused. But, recovering, she said, "Look, Willard. Like Roberta told you, Hawthorne couldn't have done this."

"On with business, huh, George? Sorry. Still, I don't think I've ever seen that many freckles."

"Willy. At a time like this? I can't believe you want to talk with me about my freckles." A soft frown made her eyes flash a brighter green.

He smiled well and long at her, which made her shift in her chair again. "Willy, I still need to get to the diner. Come on, now. Get serious."

"Why didn't you call?"

"Willy. Can we talk about that some other time?"

"When, Georgie? You never return my calls. I can't be seen hanging around your diner anymore. What did you tell me? *It'll drive customers away.'* Wasn't that it?"

"Yes."

"So, why is it that I can't talk to you anymore? Why can't we at least talk?"

"Willy." She shook her head, then stopped before speaking. "Okay. You want to do this now? For crying out loud. Okay. Okay. I don't know why, Willy. Oh, maybe because it had only been a year since Bobby died and then only four months after Vanessa passed. Goodness, Willy! I was still trying to figure things out."

"You agreed to dinner. What about that? Didn't

you have fun?"

"I had a..." She looked down at her lap. She had subconsciously locked her hands together and intertwined her fingers. "...a lovely time." She finished.

Her voice softened and deepened as she remembered how soft his lips felt when he kissed her goodnight on the neck at her car, pressing his body against hers, pinning her back against the vehicle. He felt strong. She remembered the heat coming off him as he buried his mouth in the bend of her neck. "A lovely time," she repeated and then gave a small cough.

She looked up. His mouth had turned into a half-grin and something else more virile and even less professional than before.

"Look, Willy, please. Can we get on with this?"

"Only if you promise."

"Promise what?" She nearly begged and rolled her eyes but smiled.

"Promise that after all this is over, you'll return the favor."

"What favor?"

"Well, Georgette, darn" His eyes detected movement past her, behind her through the window into the office. When she turned to look, she saw Mark ending a phone call and looking at them through the office window. It looked like he intended to come in.

"What, Willy?"

"Have me over for one of your lovely gourmet meals." He spoke fast and held up his hand to Mark outside the room, making him pause, she figured, outside the door. "You owe me a dinner."

"I owe you now, do I?"

"Come on, George. Just say yes. Don't make me

get on my knees. After all this is said and done, you're not getting back with him, are you?"

Looking down at her hands, now free of the fake ring, she didn't know what to think anymore. She agreed just to change the subject back to business.

"Okay, Willy. Okay."

He smiled like he'd won a blue ribbon and waved Mark inside.

"Mrs. Carlisle," Willard spoke again, "you know Detective Mark Dannon." When she made a face, like *of course,* he responded, "Sorry, Mrs. Carlisle, a formality is all."

"Detective." Georgette tipped her head and half-stood to shake his hand.

"Mrs. Carlisle." He took his hand back and pulled out a chair next to Willard.

"How have you been, Mark?" Georgette's face went red as she tried to recover her composure.

"The missus is about to pop."

"Another baby, Mark? Oh, well, congratulations!"

"Thanks, Mrs. Carlisle."

But Willy broke in, "Okay, enough of the niceties. How about we go over a couple of things?"

"Okay," she responded, nervous again when they returned to the issue of Helen's murder.

"The sheets." Willard referred to his notes.

"Yes." Georgette unhooked her hands, setting them on the table and scooting her chair completely under.

"You say these were your sheets. Is that right, Mrs. Carlisle?"

"Yes. That's right. They were on Helen's bed. Helen Wellen had been staying with me until she could find a place of her own."

"So, these sheets were on the bed that Helen was using at your home. Correct?"

"Correct," she reconfirmed.

His eyes looked completely serious now. "Tell me what happened with the sheets."

"Well," her voice drifted off as her mind spun back to the day she found Helen with Hawthorne. "Oh, boy. This is embarrassing."

"Don't worry, Mrs. Carlisle." Detective Mark chimed in this time. "We just want to understand how these sheets came to be used in the murder of Ms. Wellen. We're not here to judge you, Georgette."

Willard grabbed her hands in his. They felt warm and kind but suddenly turned inappropriate when Mark looked at them. She nodded slowly, pulled her hands out of Willard's grip, and continued, "I found them together." She glanced quickly to Willy, "They were, um, you know."

Willy crooked his head and squinted as if he couldn't believe what she was telling them. Then she looked back to Mark. "Helen and Hawthorne, that is." Mark sat back in his chair, lifted one foot onto his knee, and folded his arms around the other knee.

"Go on," he said in a tone that sounded like judgment to Georgette.

"Well, I kicked Helen out that day. She left within an hour, I'd say. Yes, about an hour later, she left the house. I heard her drive away."

"Did she take the sheets with her?" Willard asked next.

"No. No."

"So, how do you believe they got wrapped around Helen?"

"Well, Willy, um, Police Chief, this is what happened. I was angry with Hawthorne, as you can imagine," her eyebrows lifted, "so I stripped the bed and put them into a plastic grocery bag. I took them to the diner to fry them in hot oil or something to burn them when quite unexpectedly, he showed up."

"He?"

"Hawthorne. He came by to check on me. I wasn't about to return his calls." She looked at Willard, who looked down, understanding somehow. "So he came by. He wanted to patch things up. That's when I threw the damn bag at him."

Willy put a hand to his mouth to stifle a laugh. To hide it, he coughed instead.

Detective Mark interrupted her. "The bag with the sheets inside?"

"Yes. The plastic bag with the sheets inside." She looked at him, waiting.

"Go on."

"Oh. Okay. Well, he wanted to atone. I didn't feel like a priest right then and there," Georgette's drawl was beginning to sound more and more accentuated, "so I told him to take his rotten penance out my door and for him to go and deal with those soiled sheets. I told him to get rid of them for starters on his path to atonement."

"What happened after that?"

"He left. But, Mark. Oh, I'm sorry, I mean, Detective—"

He cut her off. "Did you hear from him after that?"

"Well. We didn't talk. He tried to contact me. But I was still refusing his calls." Again, she looked at Willy and cocked her head at him as if apologizing, and he diverted his eyes down to his notes again. Mark looked between the two of them, noticing something else was going on, but as he was looking at Willy, Willy intercepted it.

"Continue, Detective."

"So you were refusing his calls. Did he leave messages?"

"Yes."

"Do you still have these messages?"

"He left two. I deleted one but saved the other." She tried again, "But, he couldn't have—"

Again, Mark cut her off mid-sentence. "Great. We'll need to hear that recording and get records of incoming and outgoing calls from the phone company." He was talking more to Willy than to Georgette by then.

She nodded and forced out a smile.

"So, one more question, Mrs. Carlisle." She noticed the shift in formality. "You're sure you gave these sheets to Hawthorne Biggs?"

"Why, yes, Detective. Quite sure. But he couldn't have done this. He couldn't have killed or raped Helen."

Both men looked at each other, realizing Roberta revealed the lust crime part of their theory. Mark stood, shook Willy's hand, and walked out of the room. There was some sort of unspoken conversation happening between them. When Mark left, Willy turned to her.

"Did Roberta tell you about that?"

She hadn't realized the information wasn't common knowledge or how it might only be used internally for the department. "Damn." She slumped back against her chair.

"Answer me, George."

"No. One thing I know is that I don't have to answer any of your questions, Police Chief. That I'm here out of duty. I'm not a suspect, am I?" She glowered at him.

"No. You're not a suspect." He dropped the point, and they spent a few beats of clumsy silence staring at each other.

"Well, it really doesn't matter. Since you already know about that, you must know that we found zero DNA evidence, you know—semen."

But she didn't know.

"Well. That creates some trouble for you now, doesn't it?"

He tipped his head. He didn't seem to be expecting her response.

"Are we finished, Willy? I really have to go."

"Yes. We're finished, but I have to tell you this, officially, George."

"What's that?" She was standing to leave. "You can't leave town. Okay?"

"I was planning a cruise right before Helen turned up dead. I postponed it."

"Good. Just stay here. Stay available. The less you appear guilty, the better."

"Guilty! Good Lord, Willy. What are you talking about?" He stood up slowly in front of her and tried to calm her. She had forgotten how attractive he was. He looked so manly in his official dark gray dress suit.

"Shhh, George. No one really thinks you had anything to do with this, but you can't deny the love triangle aspect of this whole mess."

She rubbed both hands over her head and, in doing

so, pulled her eyes open. Then, closing them again, she dropped her arms to her sides and blew out a long worried puff of air. "Oh my goodness. This is simply tragic."

When her eyes opened again, he was looking at her.

His brown eyes remained soft and glanced from hers down to her lips, then back up to her eyes again.

"Willy, of course, I'll stay in Sunnydale. I want Helen's murderer brought to justice too."

"I know, George." He walked around the end of the table and over to her. He pulled her into him and hugged her. "I know, George. This has been a terrible, terrible time for you."

He pushed her back just inches from his chest. His pelvis and stomach smashed into her gut. He stood about five inches taller than she did. Her breasts bulged out through her T-shirt, and he seemed to examine every part of her with his eyes and with his body.

"When I can, I'll try to keep you informed as much as possible. Okay?"

She nodded, enjoying their closeness, and laying her head against his chest, she looked up at him.

He placed his warm lips on her forehead and kissed her for longer than what she thought would appear appropriate, especially in the office. She closed her eyes and let herself enjoy it.

Then his closeness became something different, something desperate.

"Oh, no." She felt him stiffen for the briefest second.

"Shhh. Don't move." She felt him draw in a deep breath, trying to strangle off his growing erection. With his breath tight in his chest, he pulled away from her slowly and, thankfully, without an erection.

Chapter 16

His wavy, ash hair looked gelled flat. Roberta was surprised he showed up. She couldn't believe his gall. He flagged her from the table where he sat eating a late dinner.

Her cell phone went off inside the pocket of her jacket. Busy-ness was always this way, in spurts. The diner was either busy or dead. Roberta now wished she hadn't agreed to Georgette taking off early, but she had been called into the police station regarding evidence surrounding Helen's death and simply couldn't stay to help with the dinner crowd.

She put a finger up to him, pulled her phone out, and showed it to him, then flipped it open and answered it. Leaning to one side, she spoke into the receiver.

"Yes? Hi, sweetheart. You'll be home, when, next Saturday? I'll do something special." She turned around and whispered in the phone to Rick, implying a promise of romance upon his return. "Okay, love you, too. Bye." She flipped the phone closed and turned around, then cashed out a waitress who had come up with someone's bill.

Roberta eyed Tanner as she counted out the change onto the tip tray. "There you go." She slammed the cash register shut, and Tanner connected with her, waving her over again.

She crossed over thirty steps or so and watched

him as he wiped his mouth on a napkin, sliding on the booth over to the wall, making room for her on his side. Roberta sat across from him.

"Hi, Martin. What's going on? I'm a little surprised to see you."

"Why is that, Roberta? I get hungry too." His dark brown eyes, the color of compost, looked dead of emotion.

"Yes, but, well," she stopped before saying too much. "What can I help you with?"

"Well, I haven't seen Hawthorne around lately and wondered if Georgette has spoken with him. I want to talk to Helen. Haven't spoken with her either since the four of us went to Chavelo's." He smiled. She couldn't read him.

"So you don't know?"

"Don't know what, Roberta?" The inflection of his words sounded practiced, and Roberta wondered why someone might go to this much trouble putting themselves in a direct line of suspicion if they were culpable of any wrongdoing.

"Helen. You don't know what happened?"

"Roberta, I just told you I haven't spoken with her in days."

Roberta looked down and then, leaning over the table making Tanner lean in too, she spoke in a whisper, "Helen, um, Martin…" He nodded, trying to look as sincere as he could. "Helen is…I'm afraid, Martin…well…Helen has died."

He pulled back, leaning against the wall, still staring at Roberta, putting on a good show. "What are you talking about?"

"I'm sorry, Martin. It's been a shock to all of us."

"Holy crap. You're serious, aren't you?"

"I'm afraid I am." She sat back against the booth as well and clutched the edge of the table. Her thumbs and fingers pinched the thickness of the table.

"I think I've lost my appetite." He pushed the plate away from him. It wasn't exactly what Roberta expected him to say, but then again, Helen and Martin, as far as she knew, had not yet been intimate. Then, he followed his show with the appropriate question. "What happened, Roberta?"

"We're not sure yet." She wasn't about to tell him anything more.

"What does that mean? Was it a heart attack, an accident? What?"

"Like I said, we're not sure. But, Martin, I'm the mayor. I really can't talk about an ongoing investigation."

"So it's being investigated."

"Martin, like I said, until we know exactly what happened, I cannot comment further."

"Of course. I understand."

"So, let me ask you, Martin, have you seen Hawthorne lately?"

He tucked in his chin, acting surprised by the question. "Like I said, not since the night the four of us went out. Why do you ask?" he said, stopping at the obvious.

"Georgette hasn't spoken with him either in a couple of days." She wasn't going to mention the affair if Tanner didn't already know.

"Oh. That's odd. No, I haven't seen Hawthorne. Haven't spoken with him. We're not that close."

Roberta cocked her head and squinted. She

remembered them talking about good old college days at the engagement party. "But, I thought you and he…"

"College, you mean?" She nodded. "Yeah, well, we kind of went our separate ways. We only recently hooked up when we met each other again at the golf club here. I moved close to Sunnydale, about twenty miles southeast of here. Sunnydale's the only decent golf course for miles. Anyway, within a week or two, so did Hawthorne. Kismet. It works in mysterious ways." She ignored the mix of clichés and agreed, nodding again and, glancing down at her hands, saw they were turning red with tension.

When she looked back up again, he was staring at her with what she could only describe as bile and hatred. She slid to the edge of the booth to get back to work and away from him.

"Sorry to have to tell you like this."

"It's awful, Roberta. Just awful."

"Yes, well, um, good night, Martin."

"Night, Roberta." He scooted his plate of food back in front of him.

Roberta walked back to the cash register to help Cammy who had taken over for her. When she got to the machine, she glanced back at Tanner. She noticed his appetite had returned. In fact, he looked ravenous.

****

Roberta's mind was still on closing the diner when she pulled her car into the Safeway parking lot. She wanted a bottle of cabernet, plus she wanted to pick up a box of scented salts for her bath tonight. She needed to unwind.

Several high-security lights beamed high above the cars, casting off what looked like misty ghosts around them. The lot was brightest closest to the concrete curb of the store. She angled her white SUV into a diagonal spot between two other vehicles. The twenty-four-hour store always seemed busy, even this late after work. As she set the gear handle into park, Roberta looked up and noted the wavy, flaxen hair, tall build, and broad shoulders of a man moving through the cars. Martin Tanner had just stepped off the curb onto the pavement and was heading toward the cars. He looked both ways as he crossed the lane between the parking spaces and the store.

She slipped down into her seat so he couldn't spot her. The engine still idled in park, but with cars pulling in and out, she didn't worry about her car making too much noise. Angling the rearview mirror to follow him, she watched as he got into a nondescript cream-colored, four-door sedan. The lights flicked on. He began to back out.

Roberta didn't know why, but she reacted rather than planning out her next few steps.

She backed out slowly and followed him, keeping her distance when he pulled off into the street. She turned the same way he turned, to the right. He stopped at the first red light as it changed to green, then continued through. Roberta, keeping about two or three car lengths between them, slowed. He drove nearly a mile, through several lights each changing as he approached an intersection, causing him to slow but not stop. He finally turned left and pulled into the hotel where they had found Helen's body.

Tanner drove around the back near a bank of high oleander hedge where a dry riverbed ran tight.

Upon turning, she had trouble locating his car. It

disappeared. She slowed down, examining each parked car as she passed by, trying to see into their dark interiors. The time since he moved out of her vision, and since she turned down the dark lot, had only been a few seconds. He couldn't have gotten out of his car and into the hotel with that little time. She assumed he was still sitting in his car, hiding.

The thought sent a cold chill throughout her body.

She hated when she began manifesting frightening scenarios. So she talked herself down. She supposed, from the many entryways lining the back of the hotel, someone in a big hurry could have made it out of their car and into the hotel without her noticing, especially if they parked right next to a door. He might've also driven around the other side of the parking lot opposite where he turned in, but why? Still, he could have.

Roberta felt a little embarrassed when she realized she wasn't really even sure if the person she saw at the market was Tanner at all.

She sped up, realizing she had let her imagination lead her there. Shaking it off, she pulled from behind the hotel and headed out, deciding she would return to the store.

Chapter 17

After returning from the store, Roberta sat for a couple of minutes in her driveway. Her house, like most others on the street, didn't have a garage. They had acreage instead. Well, a half-acre, but it provided privacy, quietness, and a sense of space in their sparsely-housed neighborhood community.

She didn't mind not having a garage. They had plenty of storage without a garage after Rick had built another storage shed in the back.

Breathing in, she realized for the first time in a long time, she could spend the night alone—enjoying a glass of wine and taking a long, hot soak in the tub. As she stood outside her car, she looked up into the sky. The storm clouds had been building and then receding all day, but the sky opened up like a kaleidoscope over her house, making the stars appear bright and almost fake. Looking northeast toward Laughlin, where Rick had moved, city lights blossomed under a massive cloud cover, killing off stars blocked by a huge gray mushroom hundreds of miles off in the distance, a cloud somehow reflecting off its darkness on an oversized truck parked on her street.

She turned again to the south, toward Phoenix. The light swelled even brighter and crossed a wider expanse down there. Phoenix also somehow reflected off the cars lined along her street, catching the shine of the city lights on them like a mirror one hundred miles away.

How is that possible? How does light power over the darkness?

Sunnydale had been her home for almost forty years, and she was thankful she didn't live in a big city any longer. Her street still felt like the country where the only lights came from the neighboring houses. In fact, they still had an ordinance forbidding streetlights at each corner. Roberta enjoyed having the night feel like nighttime. Plus, the quiet of the desert had a peace no city could equal.

Crickets sang, roadrunners cracked out calls to their mates, the wind rustled, scattering tumbleweeds, and wind chimes added the harpsichord for contrast. But there was also desert lore: if you held your breath and listened hard, you could hear the ancient natives whisper your name in the wind blowing over, rustling off the needles of saguaros. Roberta pulled in a deep breath of air, and as she held her breath, she waited, like she had since she was a kid after first hearing the story. When she let out her breath again, she said to herself, "Maybe next time, when they're ready for me to hear." The strap of the grocery bag started to cut into her hand, so she switched sides, making her switch her keys into her right hand to open the door. A breeze rustled up and blew a thin pelting of sand into her face and into the window. A bath would be a welcome respite.

Once she unlocked the door, she flipped on the light, stepped into the house, then closed the door and locked it. She could see it from where she stood, where she kicked off her pumps by the door—a note from Rick folded like a tent sitting on the counter.

She placed the bag and her keys next to the note,

pulled her jacket off, and threw it over one of the counter's bar stools. Next, Roberta opened a kitchen drawer, the one with the wine opener. A wind scudded outside, causing something to bang against the house. She looked up momentarily, trying to see if she could see out back where the noise came from, but the darkness prevented her. She pulled the wine out of the bag and grabbed his note.

He loved her. He missed her already. He couldn't wait to get home to her. He wanted to make love to her.

He drew a huge heart around the entire message and then stabbed an arrow into where it disappeared until it came out the backside again. He'd checked off three X's and drawn three O's and signed it, "Love you forever, Me."

She smiled and said in a whisper, while pouring her wine, "*I love you, too, honey.*" It didn't seem possible today. Five years ago, they nearly called it quits. He was the love of her life, no matter how trite or corny it sounded. It was true. A thought crossed her mind. She could die today and be happy.

The wind was wreaking havoc outside on the back patio, causing the lid of a trash can to fly off. She took a sip of cabernet and set the glass down.

She walked to the sliding glass door toward the back and pulled open her vertical blinds. Sure enough, the trash can had been knocked over by the wind. She looked at her watch. It was ten-thirty p.m. She had to pee and, instead of fixing the can, she walked into the guest bathroom, the one with a Jacuzzi tub, and sat on the toilet. While there, she reached over and cranked open the hot water, letting it run and build up heat. As the water ran, she thought she heard the garbage can rumbling about again. Desert wind could be violent and often brought in a host of treacheries with it, like storm clouds and gully washers. A friend of hers in Phoenix once had their roof sheer off because of the strength of the desert winds.

Flushing the toilet, she rose and pulled off her pants and panties, letting them drop to the floor. She yanked her blouse over her head and let it drop to the floor too. She grabbed Rick's robe off the hook because she liked his better. It gave her more room to dry. She headed back into the kitchen, through the den, to get her salts.

She was done in the kitchen for the evening. The garbage can could wait until morning.

She walked over toward the door to turn off the lamp. When the room went dark, a shaft of light streamed in from the bathroom, guiding her vision in its direction. Walking toward the light, something else was there, something she couldn't have described then but something she sensed, something evil. Her skin tingled, and the sensation made her want to close the blinds. She knew she got like this whenever Rick wasn't home at night with her. She shook her head, and the dark began to naturalize around her.

When she approached the pulley to close the blinds, the backyard became blocked by something darker just outside the windowed door.

Squinting to make her eyes adjust, she saw them. Recognizing both figures, she gasped.

There they were—Hawthorne and Martin— standing there, just outside her sliding glass door.

And they had guns.

Seeing them made her scream and jump back,

tripping over a chair. But she didn't fall down.

They pounded on the glass. She could see their lips moving and heard their muffled words to let them inside.

She shook her head no and darted down the hall.

The first crash of glass came as she made her way out of the living room. The sliding door opened. Both men tumbled in. Their feet pounded, running after her. She made it into her bedroom, flipped the lock, and ran over to the bed, scrambling to get to the phone. Another clatter, the door handle popping up and down with each blast. One of them bashed his shoe against the door.

It flung open wildly, slamming against the wall, then bounced back halfway.

The two men walked over to her. Hawthorne grabbed the phone and listened. She was certain he could only hear a dial tone. She hadn't had time to even call nine-one-one. A glib smile crossed over his teeth. He nodded at Tanner to check the other areas of the room. He looked in the closet and the master bath.

"Nothing."

"Better check the rest of the house."

"What the hell do you want?" Roberta tried to mask the panic in her voice.

Hawthorne didn't waste any time and backhanded her across the mouth, sending a glob of blood onto the lampshade on the nightstand. It was still dark, but she could see his eyes.

"Don't scream. Don't speak."

"You killed Helen," she croaked out, halfway crying.

He backhanded her again. "Shut up, you stupid bitch."

"She's ready, Big. Can I do her here?"

Roberta's eyes goggled in fear, understanding "do her" meant to rape her.

"You'll have time later." Then he smiled again and grabbed Roberta's face with one hand, holding her so close to his, she felt heat emanating from his mouth onto her cheek. "See, I'm your best friend right now. Believe me, what I'll do to you will seem like nothing compared to that sick freak." He tossed a look over at Tanner who was holding his crotch. "Go get a hand towel from the bathroom."

"Come on, Big, let me. She doesn't have any clothes on under that. I saw her boobs. It'd be so easy."

Roberta hadn't even noticed her robe had opened around her chest. The struggle had usurped any sense of decorum. She clutched the lapels of her robe and retightened its belt.

"What did I say? Go get a towel. Now!"

Tanner glared at her, then waggled his tongue at her like a snake, making sucking noises as he walked out of the room.

"See what I mean? I'm your only friend right now, right here. If you don't listen to me, I'll let him at you. All I have to do is step out of the room. Got it?"

She nodded her head quickly.

"Good."

When Tanner returned, Biggs took the hand towel, turning Roberta away from him. He twisted it and dropped it around her neck, making her gasp. "Grab it and stick it in your mouth." When she hesitated, he barked at her, "Do it!" She lifted the twisted towel and placed it in between her teeth. He tied it off around her head.

"Rope," he ordered Tanner, who reached into his pocket.

Roberta watched him toss over a couple of feet of thick, yellow twine. A book of matches fell out at the same time, dropping to the floor.

"Give me your hands." She shook her head no and sniveled. His hand felt like lead when he pushed her forward on the bed, making her fall on her face, pinning her there.

He lifted her robe up, revealing her bare ass, and directed Tanner, "Have at her."

Roberta thrashed and screamed as she heard Tanner unclasp his belt and his fly unzip. She writhed with her face down on the mattress as Biggs held her down with one hand, leaning all his weight on her. Her eyes went wild as she mumbled out *uh-uh* and screamed like a dog caught in a bear trap until tears soaked the bedspread.

Tanner came up fast and lay down beside her. He began petting her back and then moved his sick hand down onto her rump. "Na! Na!" she screamed, but it felt useless. She could smell his toxic breath, like garlic and bitter milk. His hand felt clammy and shook as he moved it closer to her crotch.

But Biggs stopped him. He placed one big hand on his arm and pulled him away.

"Come on, Biggs. Let me. Don't keep teasing me. You know how nasty I get when you tease me."

"Yeah, but you know how good it feels when you have to wait."

Tanner's jaw hung loose, and he laughed out a short breath. The rancid odor permeated the air around Roberta's face. "Yeah. Yeah, it does feel better when I have to wait, Big. Okay." He rolled away from her and grabbed at the front of his pants again like a boy needing to pee. "I gotta get to the bathroom."

"Now, are you going to be a good girl and let me tie your hands?"

Roberta nodded once and began to sob low and deep inside her throat. Then he turned again to Tanner. "Go get the duffle bag."

Lying face forward on the bed, she didn't see when he wound up for the blow to her head.

Chapter 18

Pressing *send*, Georgette shot an email to Roberta, describing the meeting with the police and how she thought Roberta might've slipped up when she discussed the possible rape, how Willy was still interested, which she joked about and explained details of how he got, as she typed, "aroused," adding LOL after.

Georgette assumed Roberta would be happy to hear Willy was still interested in her. Hell, Georgette was happy he was still interested. Especially in light of the whole fiasco with Hawthorne. But she wasn't going to type all of the details into the message. She knew Roberta would email back with questions.

After she pressed *send*, she leaned back in her chair and looked out the window.

Spring had fluxed toward summer except, of course, in the evenings, when the thermometer dropped thirty degrees lower than the day's temperature. Today was warmer than yesterday. The desert was on its usual uphill climb toward the inevitable scorching temperatures of summer. She had propped open both sets of French doors and cranked most of the windows open wide. The breeze crossing within the room felt fresh and clean. She loved spring and hated thinking how stifling the weather would become in just a couple of weeks, even with air conditioning with its fake cold air.

Contemplating the oncoming change in seasons, she lifted her glass of iced tea and noticed a ring puddle where it sat.

She'd only been interrupted once during her time home. Her cell hadn't even rung. Roberta would make a great partner. For the first time in the last few days, she felt content. Not quite happy, but content.

Gangster sat next to her computer where she typed and seemed fully recovered from his harrowing experience locked inside the tiny shed in the garage. Still, she gave him double the normal attention and kissed his forehead.

When her cell buzzed across the desk, it startled her. "Who's that, Gangster?" She patted his head and flipped open the phone.

It was Willy.

"Hi, Willy. Checking to see if I'm still in Sunnydale? No. Tonight is not a good night. Can we just slow up a bit on that, Willy? I mean your timing is, man oh man, I hate to say this, Willy, but your timing sucks." She couldn't believe how mean her words sounded. After she apologized, he hung up rather fast.

She tried to rationalize her rudeness—the pressure of Helen, at the very least, and the issue with Hawthorne.

With everything.

Still, she felt bad and began to dial back but then stopped. He needed to know how bad his behavior looked to her. She had been honest—rude but honest, and she refused to apologize. She made up a thousand reasons why she shouldn't apologize and knew all were weak, at best, when the phone buzzed again. She looked at the displayed number this time. It was Willy again.

"Yes, Willy." Her voice was sharp and irritated. This time Willy sounded more official. He had information about Hawthorne. They believed he had left Sunnydale under an assumed name, or maybe the name Hawthorne Biggs was a fake. His house was empty. None of his things could be found.

A cold chill snaked down her back, causing her to shiver. "What about his truck?"

"Nope. Not a car. It was a big, black, four-door pickup."

"I've never seen him in a beige sedan."

The call ended on a strange note. Willy didn't hide his hurt feelings. He talked in terse answers and sounded all business this time. Georgette couldn't help thinking this was their first lover's quarrel.

But something felt more foreboding. Willy had said they could only find one car registered to Hawthorne Biggs, and it wasn't the black truck he had been driving around.

After hanging up, she contemplated some of the points he made during their conversation. Her gut tightened when she thought about Hawthorne. She didn't really care about what truck he drove or what car he owned. Anger flared up suddenly, taking her by complete surprise.

"Dammit! The bastard lied about everything." Georgette wondered when those internal bruises would fade.

****

The diner always drew her home to it. A message blinked on the answering machine. She would get to it after looking over the books.

Georgette smiled as she reviewed business for the evening before, a bang-up dinner crowd. She was glad she and Roberta were now officially partners. Bobby's legacy would continue if anything happened to Georgette.

She stopped and made a silent prayer to her late husband, expressing how they had done well together, how much she loved his daughter, and then she got back down to work.

The evening had been busy, and she felt a moment of guilt for not being there but decided to let it go. Roberta obviously handled the night well.

She looked at the bundle of credit card receipts, noticing many of the regulars who patronized the restaurant. Friday had been busy. Today would be too. She knew she'd be tired after work tonight and couldn't wait for Sunday. They closed the doors on Sundays, and she spent her time around the house doing whatever she wanted. Still, the diner beckoned, and she knew she always felt happy to get back to it again on Monday.

But as she flipped through the credit card receipts, one of them stopped her. Roberta had written across it with a marker, *Martin Tanner was in*! She looked at the message light blinking and looked at the receipt again. Pushing her desk chair back, she rolled over to the phone to listen.

First, Roberta had decided to take the day off. She'd see her tomorrow. Georgette noticed an unusual, abrupt nature to her message.

Second, Kaplan called saying he needed Georgette to call him back, something about the contract. And when she called, the lawyer's receptionist simply stated Kaplan Hayes wanted to know if they should shred the contract or just send it to her to keep or destroy.

"What are you talking about?"

"Well, the contract. Should we destroy the original, or do you want to handle destroying it yourself?"

"Why would I want you to destroy the contract?" Georgette was flummoxed.

"Hold on, Ms. Carlisle. I'll transfer you to Mr. Hayes." While she waited on hold, she leaned forward on the desk, holding her head in one hand. Suddenly Kaplan answered, startling her from her thoughts.

"Mr. Hayes, oh, hello. Yeah, what's this about destroying the contract? Roberta called you? Reneging? No. No, I didn't know."

She felt slightly humiliated after learning from the lawyer that Roberta had canceled the contract. After hanging up with him, she dialed Roberta's cell phone, hoping to talk her out of it, but the phone went to her voice mailbox immediately as if she had it turned off. She left a message asking her to call back as soon as she got the message. She also mentioned she spoke with the lawyer and was confused by the change in plans and how they needed to talk.

Her eyes dropped to the receipt with Martin's name on it, and Georgette wondered if he knew where Hawthorne was.

By the end of the night, they had served an all-time high number of dinners. Nearly three hundred had been plated, a record night. In all the years Georgette had worked the diner, she had never seen it busier.

She fumed thinking about Roberta's decision and ripped her apron off over her head, throwing it into the laundry hamper by the bathroom door.

"Nice night to bail, Rob," Georgette grumbled to

herself. She had been irritable all night but at least the wait staff had been superb. Cammy slunk in.

"We sure could've used Roberta tonight." She said it low while she dug in her purse for a smoke.

"You're not just whistling Dixie." Georgette poured herself a glass of wine. "Want one?"

"Sure." Cammy's eyes brightened. "Let me, you know." She held up the long, slim white stick, waving it and pointing to the back door.

"I'll pour it, and you can have it when you're done." Stopping Cammy before she left, she added. "Look, will you lock up? Let the others have a glass too. Okay? If they want one. But only one, Cammy. You're in charge, okay?"

"Sure, George, but if we can only have one, will you pour my glass a little fuller?" Her broad smile eased Georgette's mind for the moment.

"Will do." She smiled back. "I'm out of here, Cam. See you on Tuesday, right?"

"Tuesday, right. Bye, George."

After draining more wine into her glass, Georgette quick-stepped up behind her and caught the back door just before it swung shut, walking through a cloud of pungent smoke from Cammy's cigarette.

"Don't take too long closing up. I can do everything with the books Monday morning. Just cash out the drawers and lock everything in the safe."

The night air glowed in yellow, misty halos around anything lighted. Rain edged even nearer. The air was steeped in faint bergamot from the humidity. It was thick with moisture, which she felt in the long, silk sleeves on her arms, from the monsoons building heavy in the south.

She heard an owl hoot low in the direction of the golf course a ways off, beyond the diner. She didn't often hear owls out there, and it stopped her right before she reached her car, making her look over in the direction of the owl. Back there, she looked in the direction of Hawthorne's house.

****

The car felt as if it were on autopilot turning down Golf Course Drive. She should've just gone straight on home, but the car led her off track. As she neared his house, she slowed and sat forward in her chair. Squinting, her vision was shredded by the darkness. His home looked abandoned, ghostly. A shudder shot across her shoulders, making the steering wheel jerk.

Where have you gone, Hawthorne? The words spoke straight from her mind, and she didn't expect an answer. Whispered out in wonderment. One minute he was in her life. The next, he had disappeared.

An odd mix of anger and worry hit her square in the solar plexus. As she drove past the empty, dark house, Georgette noticed there wasn't yet a *For Sale* sign in the yard. Pushing on the brake, her car paused in the street. She examined the shell so ominous, so empty, and so dead—like nothing had ever been alive in it before.

Spotting a cardboard sign inside the kitchen window, she squinted again to see if she could read it, but it was too far away. She backed up a few feet and then pulled her car into his drive and parked. Her heart pounded.

Leaving the motor running felt safest. She got out and stood looking around at the other houses, wondering what they might've seen in the time

Hawthorne lived there. Did Helen ever come over here with him? She placed one hand on her hip and the other over her mouth. Humiliation coursed over her, and she walked up to the window where the sign had been placed.

As she neared, closing in on it, the night's distorted letters became clearer with each step. In handwriting, the sign read, *For Rent, 928-555-1780, $750.*

"It's *a rental*."

He'd told her he owned the house but then again, he told her a lot of other things she knew weren't true. Just like the ring, all lies. She turned away and walked back to the car.

On her way home, she decided to drive past Roberta's house. The place was totally dark. Either she was sleeping, or no one was home. She'd forgotten about Rick being gone but expected Roberta to be there. Then she remembered it wasn't so late for a Saturday night. She looked at her watch—only 10:05 p.m. Maybe Roberta had gone out, or maybe she'd run to the store.

Well, Georgette wasn't about to chase her down. She would call Roberta tomorrow and talk to her then.

Chapter 19

Going to Roberta's house the previous evening and pulling back into the garage made Georgette remember how the cat got locked inside the storage cabinet. The garage's interior reeked from lack of attention, from her leaving the mess until now. And she wanted to pull the car in because the weather was turning quickly. She wasn't sure when it would rain.

With summer approaching, the winds carried a musty scent of rain, and rain in the desert not only created flash floods from water skirting across the hard pack of the desert basin, but it also created muddy window shields on cars and thick, mud-plated tires. Rains, lightning, and thunder could approach within seconds, within minutes, within hours. In the desert, rain was unpredictable.

Few mountains protected Sunnydale. The desert became a washboard of water coming directly onto its hard pack and racing over the land like a stampede of wild buffalo.

With the garage door gaping wide, fresh morning air breezed through inside, allowing the stench to circulate out.

As she tugged on a pair of rubber gloves, a clap of thunder roared nearly ten miles away, around Gray Mountain. Her hands felt dewy inside the gloves.

She picked up the blue plastic bucket. Inside it held

hot, soapy bleach water. Inside, four rags floated like drowned rats soaking in it. She pressed forward, still not wanting to deal with the chore, but she had procrastinated long enough.

The other issue she needed to broach today was the one regarding Roberta and the diner. When she pulled open the cabinet, a gust of cat urine and excrement wafted out into the expanse surrounding her. Georgette held the back of her hand to her nose, got up, and found two five-gallon buckets of used paint to hold open each door. She backed up to let out the air and replaced the back of her hand over her nose.

"Lord." The feces had hardened and moldered, the urine had crystallized to dark yellowish amber. It had seeped into the cracks where the bottom shelf attached to the side wall. She'd need a pressure sprayer to really get it clean.

"Oh, man." She thought about postponing the job again but knew no time was ever good for a job like this one. Picking up six pieces of hard, dry droppings with some paper towels, Georgette crumpled the paper tight and got up from her knees to throw the entire mess into the garbage can.

When she got back to the cabinet, she noticed the corner of an envelope on the second shelf from the top, but it didn't register in her mind to be anything necessarily important, so she went back to the duty of washing up the cat's urine.

Dropping back to her knees, she squeezed out one rag and looked at the bottom metal shelf. She set the rag onto it and wiped. The hardened urine felt like scraping sugar under the cloth. She scrubbed, trying to dissolve it, and folded the towel into quarters each time to find a new clean side. Each time, the rag tugged against the urine spot like sandpaper. She set the rag outside the bucket on the ground and pulled out another one. The shelf glistened, and she sat waiting for just a couple of seconds, hoping the sandy-textured urine would soften. She looked up at the second shelf again, subliminally noticing the white corner of the envelope, then wiped the back of her hand across her brow, pulling some hair out of her eyes. Lifting the new rag out and wringing it, bleach water slopped up and splattered her T-shirt and face. She wiped at her shirt, noticing streaks of yellow instantly.

Looking back at the bottom shelf, she leaned into the cabinet, wiping more rigorously. The urine had broken up. She folded the rag into quarters and continued wiping. Each swipe felt smoother than the last.

After setting the rag on the ground with the other used one, she grabbed and wrung out one more. But leaning back this time, her eyes connected with the envelope sitting just above her head. She didn't take her eyes off the letter but continued to clean, leaning in and wiping, recognizing this must've been one of Helen's documents.

Pausing for a moment, she raised up on her knees. The note had HW/GC written across the front of it. Her mind drifted to Roberta. She never imagined Roberta would've bagged on their partnership without talking to her about it first. The thought burned her eyes, making her stop, which caused her to sit back fully on her heels and squeeze her eyes shut.

When she opened them, she couldn't ignore the letter anymore. HW/GC. Their initials—Helen

Wellen/Georgette Carlisle.

The shelf which had housed the cat would be fine for now. If it continued to smell in there, she could always clean it out again later.

Pushing herself up into a stance, her legs warmed as the blood flowed back down through them into her calves and ankles. She peeled off her rubber gloves and slung them over the lip of the wash bucket. After examining the envelope, she lifted it, turning the thing over in her hands and, checking the back of it, she saw Helen had folded the lip inside the opening.

She figured this was one last drama for Helen. So, folding the envelope in half, she shoved it into her back pocket, set her cleaning supplies outside the garage, and pulled her car back in.

After making sure the garage door closed and didn't bump back up and reopen, she dumped the soiled water onto some rocks along the side of the driveway. Forgetting about the rags, they went slopping out.

"Damn." Picking them up off the driveway, she felt a tug against her ass where she had filled her back pocket with Helen's letter. She mustn't forget to read it later.

The temperature had risen since only a half hour before. She looked up and caught the edge of a towering, bulbous, leaden cloud climbing over the roof of her home.

The air had changed also, had become like a greenhouse—humid and hot.

A light drizzle had fallen onto her arms and shoulders, causing them to glisten. Another clap of thunder rang deep through the desert, resounding under the bell jar created by the bowl of clouds over the land.

Rain was falling somewhere. She walked around the side of the house to look.

A wide sheet of water poured like a thick tongue hanging out of a huge, gray mouth the clouds were making. Too much water falling onto the dry desert floor was always cause for concern. Too much rain can give way to torrential flooding, flash floods they call them, when so much rain washes away loose earth.

****

Cracking open a beer, Georgette angled out a chair, sat at the kitchen table, and pulled her dirty T-shirt over her head. In only her bra, she shook out her strawberry hair from her ponytail and stared at the table. There the folded envelope sat, looking plain and harmless.

Gangster jumped up onto the chair before she could sit. "You little monster." She picked him up and nuzzled his neck, then she set him on the table and reclaimed her seat. The cat lay in a heap across the tabletop and the envelope, like royalty.

"You don't want me to work, do you? You want Mommy to play with you today."

She rubbed his head, sliding her hand under his jaw and scratching his chin. He pressed up again on all fours and leaned into the attention. When he did, Georgette snatched the letter out from under him and took a slug of beer.

"Okay. What now?" Pangs of anger still arose in Georgette even with Helen dead.

Scanning it quickly, partly to herself, partly aloud, she came to his name and then stopped. Commenting openly now, she sounded confused. "Zach Pinzer?"

Pausing momentarily, she grabbed up her beer bottle again and took another deep swig. "What the hell? Zach Pinzer?" She couldn't fathom why Helen would be writing about him.

She started rereading the note from the top. Helen's writing had been scrawled in a jumble of letters flowing from one word into the next. Each letter looked rushed, almost panicked. Georgette read her words as a declaration of sorts, somehow a confession from her—another one.

But was she reading this correctly? Was there some sort of interaction between Helen and Zach? Reading it again, yes, there had been something about the diner. Helen would get half the ownership and...Pinzer? The other half!

"What the hell?"

No one but family had any rights to half of her diner, and her only family was Roberta. The words in Helen's note tumbled from her mouth as she read.

Her eyes tightened, trying to understand. Then she saw another name—Hawthorne. He had been involved as well, but as Helen was stating—if Georgette was reading the note correctly—only *after* Helen's involvement. She felt totally off-balance and confused now.

George,

What is it about us? About me?

When he contacted me, I was so desperate. Have you ever been desperate, George? If you have, well, maybe you can understand me, if only a little.

You must realize what a weak woman I am by now. Pathetic. I'm embarrassed by my past, my thoughts, my actions. You're my most precious friend, and this is what I do? Betray you? I don't know why. I have no answers. All I'm left with is remorse.

Once Zach put the plan into my head, it actually sounded like a good idea. Then, the threat of silence or death if I didn't keep quiet. So, I agreed.

We would get you to give me or sell me the diner "for a song," as he put it. Then, he would take care of the rest. He would get half; I would get the other half. He said if I tried anything funny, if I didn't relinquish the diner to him afterward, he would somehow implicate me in your death.

I can't believe I had a hand in any of this. That I actually began a liaison with this man in this plan, a plan where you would end up dead. Of course, the ridiculous part is that he intended to kill me too. Of course he did. It was a deal with the devil—my life or my soul—either way, I lost.

The thing is, my life started folding in on itself. I couldn't look into my own eyes anymore. I couldn't sleep. My mind wouldn't stop fretting about the egregiousness of our plan. So, I backed out and wrote him a letter to that effect. I refused to go through with it. And then, I ran. I figured he wouldn't ever believe I would return to his city or Sunnydale. Why would I, right?

But then I met Hawthorne. I hadn't been with a good man since before Harold. I was so lonely. And when he started to flirt with me and then acted on it, well, I thought I had been rewarded somehow, by God, maybe, I don't know. Then I overheard him outside my hotel room door on the phone with someone. They were supposed to "do away with that Pyle woman," as he put it.

And, even though Martin whispered the words, they sounded like someone screaming them out of a bullhorn. I watched them through my peephole as the two of them discussed my death. That's when I realized Zach had located me, and Hawthorne had become my replacement in his plans.

It's all my fault. If I had never agreed to this, well, I don't know.

All I know is that I'm dreadfully sorry for my part in this crime. Please find some way to forgive me, George. I can't live knowing you...

The letter trailed off there and had not been signed. Her penmanship was terrible but definitely identifiable as Helen's—to Georgette at least. The last sentence had no period, adding to the rushed feel of the entire correspondence.

Slamming the letter onto the table, she felt her face redden. The cat's ears splayed back at the abrupt noise.

"Can you flipping believe this, Gangster?" She shook the letter at him, and he dived off the table.

Lifting the phone, she dialed Roberta again. The phone rang but clicked over to the recorded message. She didn't bother to leave one.

She looked at the clock on the wall. It was before noon. She couldn't believe Helen's involvement with Zach Pinzer. She picked up the beer bottle again. It was half-empty. Putting it up to her mouth, she wondered how they had ever connected. She shook her head in disbelief. What did they actually plan on doing? How were they going to kill her to get the diner?

Georgette didn't even feel the bottle slip from her fingers. She only heard it exploding into shards on the cold Saltillo kitchen floor.

They had killed Helen for it. They'd locked Gangster inside the cabinet.

They would go to any lengths, murder, rape—anything to take ownership of her land.

When she jumped up, the chair screeched across the tile, sending Gangster bounding off the table. "OhmyG—Roberta!" It wasn't like her not to pick up her calls or not return messages.

She dialed her number again. Nothing.

Running into her bedroom, she yanked open her top drawer—her panty drawer where she hid her .38—the one she hid under her red satins. But when she shifted them, the gun wasn't there. She moved to the other side of the drawer. Maybe she'd forgotten and put it under the black ones. But no, her gun wasn't there either. Pulling the entire drawer out, she dumped the contents onto her bed.

Pulling each of the six drawers out, she dumped each onto the bed. She ripped open her closet door and scrambled up on a footstool, sweeping her hand across the length of the upper shelving. There were only her purses and luggage. She slid all of them off onto the floor and got down. Searching each bag, she tossed them out of the closet, one by one, onto the bedroom floor.

It wasn't anywhere. Her gun was gone.

The tires laid a patch of rubber four feet long on her driveway as Georgette pulled out. Her car lurched as she threw the gear from reverse into drive.

The change from a dead stop to speeding made the tires scream again, probably leaving more rubber on the street behind her.

She had to get to Roberta's house. This wasn't like her, not calling. It certainly wasn't like her to not show up for work. And why would she have canceled the contract?

Pulling across the highway, she zipped in between two cars, one coming from the north, one heading south. Her car heaved across the median, causing her ass to lift off the seat a good six inches over each trundle. But this way was a straight shortcut to Roberta's house over on Gold Miners Road. She had no time to turn right on Highway 93 a mile away, where making a U-turn was legal but time-consuming, and then to head back south again.

The car creaked and clamored, hitting the curb, chucking up, then banging down on the other side, and reconnecting onto the opposite road's pavement. Someone honked out a loud, long whine of annoyance. She didn't even look.

"Roberta," she snarled out, halfway crying, halfway angry.

It seemed as if her cell phone was hiding from her as Georgette searched her purse contents with one hand, driving recklessly with the other. The bag was useless and too deep for emergencies.

A gust of wind blew in, flicking at her hair and causing her flouncy garnet-colored smock to lift out like a tent around her torso.

Turning too fast, she felt the car leaning into a curve, and she hoped she wouldn't skid out. Pulling the steering wheel to correct it, she clipped a mailbox, sending it off its base and denting the right edge trim of the window. Her car skidded to a stop in front of Roberta's house. She'd settle the issue of the mailbox later.

Running up to the front, she reached the door and banged on it, screaming Roberta's name. The house seemed lifeless.

She moved over to the kitchen window and, cupping her hands onto the glass, peered inside. No one.

Then, she banged on the window calling Roberta's name. She ran around the back of the house, through their gate to the side window where Roberta and Rick's bedroom was.

She banged on the window. "Roberta! It's George. You here?"

Her screaming had turned dire. Her throat closed around each word.

Georgette ran to the back but stopped.

She stood there frozen, not believing what she saw.

The glass sliding door had been broken into. It looked like someone had kicked a hole through it; it hung off its tracks, and a long, single crack ran from one corner at the bottom diagonally all the way to the top.

"Oh, please, Lord." She hadn't heard from Roberta since Friday. It had been two days.

Chapter 20

When Willy showed up with the crime scene unit, Georgette was sitting on a chair on Roberta's front porch.

"Willy, what are we going to do?"

"Georgette, look, you're no good here. We can only do so much. Why don't you go home and wait."

"Wait! Willy, she's my daughter!"

He tipped his head. His eyes warmed and softened at her statement.

Everyone in town knew Roberta was the daughter of Bobby, but since Vanessa died, Georgette felt like Roberta was her own.

Georgette still understood when people saw them together. Their age difference made them appear more like sisters than anything else. But she didn't care. The age difference was only a technicality. Roberta, in Georgette's mind, was her daughter.

Her heart raced, and her chin fluttered while she stared at Willy, expecting him to do something more.

"George." He pulled her into him. "Look, she's special to me too."

As he held her, she began to cry. "I promise you. We'll find her. Okay?" He pulled her back to look into her eyes. She sniffled and wiped at her nose.

"Okay?" he repeated.

Georgette nodded yes. "Okay, Willy. But you

promised. Remember that. You promised."

She turned and continued to wipe at her face until she reached her car. Before getting back in, she looked over its hood and mouthed the words back to Willy. *"You promised me."* She noted how his face looked old then. He looked serious and faithful.

Driving off, she refused to go home. Being at home would only serve to send her into the land of the loonies. Instead, she wanted to get a bottle of wine. She drove through the residential area surrounding Roberta's house and exited out Country Club Road, which intersected with Highway 93, where there was an all-night grocery store.

She wanted to stop there first and take some time to decide what else she needed to do. While idling at the stoplight, she prayed to her late husband, Roberta's dad. "Oh, Bobby. God? You there? Please help me. I didn't mean to lose your daughter, Bobby. Please let her be okay. Please."

She openly cried quietly inside the car. The hum of her engine in the background and the moaning coming from her sounded weak and helpless.

When the light changed from red to green, she wiped a sleeve across her nose. She looked toward the store sitting kitty-corner from where she was in the right-hand lane. Beyond the light sat a massive median. With no chance to make a left turn into the store, Georgette turned right, south on 93. She would make a U-turn, reroute, and turn right into the store's parking lot off Highway 93.

As she drove south, she noticed someone who looked familiar in the parking lot of the hotel where they had found Helen. He maneuvered a large duffle bag he was rolling. Already in the left lane, she cranked her neck and thought the man looked a lot like Martin Tanner, but she had to turn left by then.

When she pulled the one-eighty back onto 93, she tried to see if the man was still in view, but she'd lost him behind a few cars.

Staying in the left lane, she decided to turn around again. Passing through the light, her heart began palpitating. She breathed in and out, trying to settle herself, but she felt a surge of adrenaline pulse through her body and couldn't control the onset of shakes.

By then, her tears had dried, and the car seemed to drive itself.

She reached inside her purse. This time her hand landed, magically enough, on her cell. Georgette remembered she'd forgotten to mention her missing gun to Willy. She needed to call him back. Looking down and flipping open the phone, she nearly tail-ended the car in front of her. It had stopped for the light. She skidded to a stop inches before connecting. It would have been a disaster. If she had gotten into an accident, the time spent dealing with insurance and the police could've meant the difference between finding Roberta alive and finding her dead.

Pressing Willy's cell number, she listened for him to answer.

Clouds built just miles beyond the mountains, and with the wind pushing like it was now, the storm would be hitting within an hour, she figured.

As Willy answered, a flash of lightning scudded across the sky for miles, splitting the eastern sky, looking as though the charcoal thunderclouds were chasing the flash behind it.

"Willy," she said when the recording sounded in her ear. Then realizing it wasn't Willy, she stopped speaking until the phone beeped, then said, "Call me back. I think I just spotted Martin Tanner. He knows Hawthorne. Call me back."

Flipping the phone closed again, she realized she had forgotten to mention the note to Willy. When he called her back, she would remember to tell him about her missing gun and Helen's note—a confession and explanation incriminating other accomplices.

****

Thirty-six hours slithered by with Roberta's strength dwindling. The small room smelled like burnt coffee and old pizza. Her left eye had swelled badly from being punched. She could only manage to see through a squint. But it was difficult to keep either eye open by now.

She feared if she fell asleep, Tanner would get to her.

Her head dipped, and a thin veil fell over her mind, something one might describe as sleep, but when Tanner spoke, she forced herself awake.

"He should've called by now."

Ignoring him, Biggs shrugged his arms tighter around himself. He, too, had been drifting in and out of consciousness. Tanner, with a constant eye on Roberta, looked like the only one out of the three who didn't seem tired. In fact, he appeared on high alert, even jittery. He had been drinking an inordinate amount of coffee. Roberta had, too, and so had Biggs, but yet, they were on the verge of exhaustion while Tanner seemed ready to jump out of his own skin.

The blackout curtains of the scrubby motel room

created the sensation of nighttime, but Roberta had been trying to watch the clock since she'd been abducted. It was daytime now, although she would never have known that because of the curtain and the blindfold from which she could only see a sliver when she looked at the floor.

A low rolling rumble, sounding like a storm coming, rose and fell somewhere outside. She imagined standing outside to see the sky fill with rain clouds, to be untied, free from her captors.

Tanner rose, antsy and hoping to get at her, approaching as he walked toward the kitchen for another cup of coffee. Biggs had the TV on and was slipping in and out of consciousness again.

She'd been sitting in a hard wooden kitchen chair for hours. Her ass had gone from aching to numb. She preferred the pain. At least she felt alive when her hips ached. The numbness, however, made her feel dead all over.

When Tanner walked past her, he brushed an open hand across her breast, bent down fast into her face over her shoulder, and stood behind her.

He gripped her breast hard and tight and talked to her so close that she could smell the bitter coffee off his tongue.

"*He can't stay awake forever,*" he whispered in her ear, the heat of his breath burning her skin. He tipped his head to Biggs. She moaned in a high pitch through the rag they'd stuffed into her mouth.

Biggs, with his arms crossed over his chest and one foot on, one foot off the sofa, spoke in a surgical tone. "Leave her alone, Tanner."

He kept his eyes closed. Roberta twisted her body

out of his grip. He dug into his jeans pocket, pulled out a small tin, and walked off. Roberta cranked her neck around to make sure she was a safe distance from him. With his back to her, he slipped open the tin and shook it once. Then, throwing his head back, he popped whatever he had in the tin into his mouth. She assumed, from his agitated state, he was taking amphetamines.

He turned quickly to look at her and then again, like a snake, fluttered his tongue at her. It sickened her, and she didn't hide her feelings.

"I'm telling ya, Biggs, he should've called by now."

In the last day and a half, the two men worked out the situation together. Someone else above them was calling the shots via phone conversations Hawthorne received. He had gotten a call on Saturday at one o'clock. They expected another call again today within the hour, at one o'clock.

"Shut up." Hawthorne shot a quick peek at Roberta as she focused on both men again. She hadn't meant to sleep.

Roberta said, "I need to pee."

"I'll take her."

"Shut the hell up," Biggs barked at Tanner.

"You let me with Helen."

"That was different."

"Why?"

"She threatened me. Plus, Helen wasn't the God-blessed mayor, asshole. Now shut up, and if he calls while we're in the toilet, keep talking to him until we get back."

Roberta understood they meant Helen had been raped. Since Biggs had slugged her, she had remained quiet, only speaking when they asked her questions and when they forced her to leave those two scripted messages, one to Kaplan Hayes and the other to Georgette.

As Biggs untied her arms from behind the chair, she tried to remember each conversation, trying to puzzle everything together.

They wanted to obtain ownership of the diner, clearly, but why? And who was the man on the phone? She figured the "why" part of the equation was out of greed.

That part was simple too.

They'd double-tied her, once around her wrists, then again onto the chair. Biggs raised her from the chair by yanking up on her arms, forcing her to stand. "Let's make this one quick." She nodded fast. "You know the drill." He pulled the blindfold up to her forehead. She turned around like she had all the other times. Her whole skull felt bruised.

The time before when she urinated, she fell asleep leaning back against the toilet. Biggs had fallen asleep on the couch, allowing Tanner to sneak in. But when he touched her, she awoke and began kicking him and screaming.

Hawthorne raced in and dragged him off her, and then he flung him out the bathroom door like a schoolboy. She wouldn't make the same mistake this time.

They didn't hear her finish, and walking back out from the toilet, she had a view of the entire room. Both guns sat several feet away from her chair on the dresser near the TV, next to Biggs's cell phone. The duffle bag lay on the bed, gaping open.

Her jaw was sore. Keeping her mouth open like this had put an unusual amount of strain on her facial muscles.

The phone jangled, making Biggs rise and swing his feet down, and Tanner raced to answer it, spilling coffee onto the floor as he moved from the kitchen over to the dresser.

"Hey," Tanner answered the phone, then turning, he handed the phone to Biggs. Roberta had seen the roles playing out this way quite often. Tanner was Biggs's boy. And Biggs? Owned by the guy phoning in.

"Yeah." He listened dutifully. "Where?" He stopped for more instruction. "Got it." He ended the call. "Wants us to move. Says we've been here too long."

"Where?"

Biggs rolled his eyes and tipped his head toward Roberta. They wouldn't say in front of her.

"Get her in the bag."

It hadn't even occurred to her how they got her into the hotel without being seen. The duffle bag had been her most recent mode of transportation.

They tied Roberta to the chair again. She flailed and moaned but couldn't get any volume because of the gag in her mouth. She rocked the chair, trying to somehow unleash herself. It was a primal urge—her body, its reaction, thrashing, groaning, crying. Her fear peaked when she thought no one might even realize she was missing.

"Don't make me hurt you, bitch." Tanner, smiling, showed no anger. He walked up in front of Roberta, who had not yet calmed down.

Biggs, now standing, put his cell phone in his pants

pocket and walked calmly to the dresser, retrieving his and Tanner's guns.

"Shut her up," was all Biggs said. It took only one punch, this time to the right side of her jaw, to knock her out.

Chapter 21

"We found something, Boss." Taylor West, dressed in chalk-line blue from neck to toe, was one of Willy's men at the scene.

He held up an evidence baggie between his gloved fingers. The sanitary gloves stretched tight across the tips, allowing his fingernail bed to show through. He rubbed his nose, clearing the oil off his nut-brown skin. His fifties-style, black-rimmed glasses didn't do justice to his good looks.

"A few hairs too, found a partial and tons of full sets from what I gather are Roberta's and Rick's."

Willy eyed the baggie and its contents. "Any writing on it?"

"Nope."

"Where's it from?"

"The Sunnydale ESL on Highway 93."

"Where they found Helen Wellen?"

"Same one."

"Sound like a coincidence to you, West?"

"You know what they say about coincidences, Boss?"

"No, what's that?" Willy egged on his answer.

"There aren't any."

"And the partial?"

"Yep. I want to get it to the lab and run it through Solaris."

"Good. I want that info now. Go. Call as soon as you know something."

West turned to leave the scene with the matchbook. He wiped at his forehead and adjusted his glasses closer to his face on the bridge of his nose. "It's muggy today," he called back, unzipping his blue clean suit. "Muggy and hot."

Willy looked out across the horizon, seeing a mountainous thundercloud billowing in the east. "Looks like rain in the mountains. Know what that means."

"Idiot drivers trying to surf!" West yelled back as he walked, holding up the hand with the baggie, acknowledging Willy.

"Call as soon as you know!" Willy called out again.

"Check, Boss." Willy jumped into the white police van and sped off.

On the outside, Willy remained calm. But his heart pounded inside his chest.

The scene showed obvious signs of violence—from the back window being busted out to a trail of destruction through the house and blood in the master bedroom. He feared the worst—they had found blood on the bed and splatter on the lamp, blood he assumed was Roberta's.

His exterior spoke of authority and finesse while inside, he feared for Roberta and the injuries she had incurred, or worse—her possible brutal murder.

He resolved to wait on another call to Georgette. Alarming her any further wasn't the way to handle things. He had to remind himself this wasn't personal, even though in their small town, he had personal relations with so many folks. It was hard not to become close with each and every crime.

****

She swung her car into the hotel's parking lot, watching to see if she could spot the man with the duffle bag. If it had been Hawthorne, if he was culpable in any of this murder business with Helen, he was hiding in plain sight. Just like him to be brazen.

Her arms cranked the wheel, straightening out the car as she drove behind the building instead of where she saw the man's car.

Parking now, she stopped to decide on some plan of action while the car idled.

Behind the hotel, the wall of oleanders wagged wild in the breeze from the storm pushing closer. Behind the bank of oleanders, a glint of something shiny and dark caught her attention. She shifted the gear down again and drove closer to the hedge, then parked, letting the car idle again. She got out and stepped nearer to a shallow, dry riverbed running just parallel to the shrubs—the same riverbed curved and twisted northeast toward the coming storm. Placing her hands between some limbs, she pressed the branches open.

Hawthorne's big, black truck sat empty down in the narrow channel. It was all the proof Georgette needed—him hiding there.

She knew he had killed Helen, and now he had Roberta.

Making her way back to her car, she remembered she had no way to protect herself. Looking for anything, she pulled open the glove compartment. Scraping out its contents and finding nothing, she sat back and stopped to think.

Using the car's interior control, she popped open the trunk and jumped out fast. Lifting the trunk open, she pulled out her emergency kit with the flare gun inside, pressed the trunk closed again, and got back to safety inside her car. She angled around, looking for anyone who might have witnessed her. When it appeared no one had, she unlatched the box and pulled out an even smaller box.

Her heart pounded when she considered what she might have to do. But if it meant she might save Roberta, well then, she would do anything. The cardboard lid squealed when it came off.

She flicked the small latch, and holding the handle in her left hand, she loaded one thick, oversized red signal into the flare gun's chamber. Closing it, she pocketed another flare. She noticed the box stated the flare gun's five-hundred-foot projectile capability. "*Okay*," she whispered. She was plenty far away to maintain a safe distance from Hawthorne.

Turning toward the steering wheel again, she turned off the car and started to get out but stopped. She looked again at the other two flares in the box, snatched them both, and stuffed them into her other pocket.

****

Tanner regained the duty of rolling the oversized, heavy duffle bag from the hotel room to the car. Stopping at the elevator, they waited, each looking up at the lights striking numbered floors. A maid's cart clanged down the hall after pulling out from a room she had recently cleaned.

"Did you put the *Do Not Disturb* sign on the door?" Biggs spoke low.

"Dammit to hell."

"You moron. They don't need to find our gun ever, and if they do find one, not until after we're long gone. Give me the key, you retard."

Biggs held his hand out when the elevator chimed and swooshed open. "You get Georgette's piece?"

Tanner tried not to act flustered, tapped his pocket, and nodded about the gun, then said, "Here," handing off the handle to Biggs. "I'll get it and catch the next one. Go on."

An elderly woman, leaning on an oversized black umbrella like a cane, stood inside the elevator, smiling as she held the doors open with the button.

"Going down?" she said, almost yelling to them after waiting for them to come in.

"Yes, ma'am. Just *uno momentito*." Biggs winked at her, making her cloudy eyes almost disappear in a wrinkle from smiling.

"See you down there." Tanner walked off, reversing his steps toward their room.

Biggs tugged the heavy bag into the elevator, pivoting it around, so it was beside him, away from the woman.

"Looks like rain," she said.

"Does it? Haven't been out today."

He felt the bag move. He coughed to distract the woman. Roberta moaned inside.

"I'm sorry?" she said.

"Haven't been outside," he spoke loudly, realizing the woman's hearing was impaired.

"Oh, my, it's absolutely gorgeous today. Even with the storm coming." Her soprano voice warbled from age.

He whispered low to check for sure. "You're an

old bat, aren't you?"

She turned and smiled when the elevator bottomed out. Roberta moaned again, pressing against the wall of the bag. He kicked it to shut her up and stop her wriggling.

"Take care." She clomped her umbrella in front of each step and shuffled toward the lobby.

"Yes, ma'am." He spoke so loud, the young Korean reservation clerk, Lisa, looked up at him and smiled.

"Hello, Mrs. Reynolds." Lisa turned her attention to the old woman, and Biggs turned the other way toward the double glass doors.

Pushing through, he tugged against Roberta's weight in the duffle bag. She groaned audibly. He looked down and saw the green canvas move as she writhed inside it. He pulled over away from the glass doors, away from anyone's view, and punched the bag where he knew Roberta's face was. He only heard a huff, and then the movement stopped. "Stop moving, bitch, or you're dead." He spoke only inches from the bag, acting as if he were tying a shoelace.

When he stood, he reached in his pocket and pulled out the keys to their battered beige sedan, the one with no license plates. And rolling the bag again, he walked to the car.

With his key in the trunk lock, he looked up and saw Georgette's car. He worried she might be looking toward the hotel, so he lifted the trunk lid for cover. He peeked out and saw her. She was heading toward the hotel.

He shoved the retractable handle of the duffle bag into itself and waited behind the trunk for Tanner to come out and help. Just as he turned to the hotel doors, Tanner pushed through them.

He had thought enough to put on his sunglasses and golf cap. After seeing Georgette, Hawthorne wished he had done the same as well.

Chapter 22

"So what is it?"

"It's only a seven-point match, but we think it belongs to Mister Melvin Taggert."

As Willy sat in his police car, he listened and jotted down notes while he talked with West through the hands-free car phone. "Now, who the hell is Melvin Taggert?"

"Some career con. In and out of Florence on some offense or another. He has a juvenile sheet. From what I can tell, mostly for battery charges. There's one sexual assault with a seventeen-year-old. He pled out and admitted he had sex with her but said she consented. She said it was rape. He got five years. Just released about six months ago."

"What's he look like?"

"Forty-five, average build, sandy hair, five-eleven, one-ninety."

"Damn. I was hoping for prints on Biggs."

"Yeah. Still nothing on Hawthorne Biggs. Searched CODIS too. Nothing. He's a no-name. Probably made up."

Willy noticed the cell on his passenger seat blinking. He'd missed a call.

"Okay. Good work, West."

"Thanks, Boss."

"One more thing. Will you go check on Georgette

Carlisle for me? At her house? She's not at the diner today."

"Sure thing, Boss. Why should I say I'm calling on her?"

"Tell her we have a lead, but that's all."

"Will do."

"Thanks, West. Bye."

He pressed the off button on the phone and got out of his car but didn't close the door. Poking his head above the hood, he called out to the other investigators.

"I'm going to check on something. I'll be back." He sat back down and, turning on his car, grabbed his cell phone and dialed to listen to his messages. He had only one—from Georgette. He slid his pencil above his ear and flicked on the radio. A local newscaster was predicting a severe flood. They reported the news onsite out west of the Grays.

Willy felt for his pocket where he used to keep his cigarettes. He pulled the pencil from behind his ear and placed it between his lips. He hadn't smoked in years. As he turned off Roberta's street, his heart thumped hard inside his chest.

****

Roberta noticed the dark first, then her sore jaw. The gag wedged between her teeth for so long had chafed the corners of her mouth into raw, seeping wounds.

Bound like a pig, she felt the cool plastic zipper of the duffle bag against her cheek. She remembered they had closed her up inside the bag, zipping it up over her head.

A sense of claustrophobic nausea swept over her, and she panicked. She thrashed against the strain of the leather bag, but when she did, she felt the ligature around her neck tighten.

****

Mrs. Reynolds spent every spring in Sunnydale. Never traveling too far from Phoenix, she still enjoyed getting out of the hustling sprawl of the big city. She'd been coming to Sunnydale now for thirty-seven years. The first time visiting, Mr. Reynolds had joined her, but only two years later, he died. Now, at age eighty-four, Mrs. Reynolds spent her time in the higher desert alone, reminiscing about her life before. It was Mr. Reynolds who had given her a lust for the desert and all its unpredictability.

Tapping her umbrella in rhythm with each plodding step as she walked away from the reception desk, she decided to take in some fresh air. Even with the storm approaching, she would still enjoy sitting out under the gazebo amid the small, flowering, landscaped yard positioned near the entrance of the hotel's parking lot. She would be able to watch the approaching storm vividly from there through her aging eyes, eyes once gleaming sharp sea green, so green her husband used to say he wanted to skinny dip in them. Her eyes were now hazy seafoam green from so many years gone by.

As she walked, she leaned against her long umbrella, stopping every three steps or so to catch her breath.

Tanner, strapping himself into his car seat with the old-fashioned lap belt, stopped when he heard a noise emanating from the trunk. He and Biggs stared at each other without speaking for a single moment before they both heard the noise again.

"The bitch is awake. She's gonna kill herself like

that."

"Let's get out of here. We can dump her body on our way to the city."

Tanner pulled his seatbelt snug across his hips. He tugged at the legs of his jeans, adjusting himself before they pulled out of the hotel parking lot.

"You promised me, Biggs. I get a go at her, right?"

"She'll be dead in a few minutes."

"Sometimes it's better that way." Tanner wiped a gob of spittle from the corner of his mouth.

"Whatever, you sick bastard."

It was raining hard over the mountains now, and a jagged lightning bolt coursed through the sky as Georgette skulked over to the side of the hotel. Looking out at the row of cars parked tight—each nearly on top of the next—she saw the beige one she spied Hawthorne at earlier.

Feeling for the flare gun in the waistband of her pants, Georgette patted at her loose blouse, determining if the gun could be seen. The handle poked out just over her belt, but it was mostly hidden. A gust of wind made a creosote shrub rustle and slap her in the face. When she recovered, the men had returned to the car. They looked like they were leaving. Tanner split off toward the passenger side and Biggs to the driver's side. When Tanner passed by the trunk, he patted it and leaned in, putting his face so close it appeared he said something, something Georgette couldn't quite hear.

She turned back and ran to her car, intending to follow them, when a howling rack of thunder uncoiled across the sky, stopping her cold.

****

Willy chewed on his pencil, slicing up the yellow

paint and digging into the wood with his teeth until it snapped in two at the graphite's core. He spat one end out of his mouth and was tossing the other onto the floor of his police car when the call came in.

The scratchy squeal of the CB arced and hummed until a woman's voice, Meg's, came over the radio. "Police Chief?"

Willy lifted the radio's speaker. "Yep, here."

"We have a situation, sir."

"What kind of situation?" Willy had turned the wheel toward Highway 93.

"Well, sir, it seems some yahoo decided to try and cross the gully." Her voice made it sound like a question, but it wasn't a question.

"Uh-huh."

"With his horse trailer that sunk into the wet silt on the edge of the gully?" She paused.

"Yes, Meg, and..." His mood, his voice, meant business.

"Well, sir," she quickened the pace of her speech. "He's stuck in the gully, and the water is rising. Newscasters have called, saying he's gonna drown if someone doesn't do something."

"Crap Almighty."

"Good news, though, sir—"

"Yeah, what's that?"

"The horse is safe."

"Okay. Dispatch Sunnydale Fire Department. I'll meet them there. But, Meg—"

"Sir?"

"Where's Mark?"

"Baby's on its way. Got the call about an hour ago. He's at the hospital."

"Crap fire." He rolled his eyes and shook his head. "You know what, Meg?"

"What, sir?"

"Timing is everything."

"Yes, sir. I believe that's right, sir."

"Call the FD. I'll meet them at the gully."

"Yes, sir. Over, sir."

He switched on the car's flashing lights, flipped on the siren, and pulled the car into a full turn in the opposite direction, pressing hard on the gas.

****

Breathing in short and quick pants, trying to relax and loosen the grip of rope around her throat, Roberta felt a nub and knew it was the backside of the pull-tab of the zipper. She nosed it to see if it would move. When it did, she worked slowly at first, making sure the cinch around her neck wouldn't tighten. It hadn't.

Moving her legs seemed the only thing making the noose constrict. Forcing her back against the bag, she added just the right amount of pressure to work the small nub.

A preoccupation with the thought she might get free from the duffle bag took her mind off the fact these two men were going to kill her if she didn't escape. So escaping was her only option.

She continued working the top of the zipper with her nose, moving it only a millimeter every time. And each time she jimmied the zipper, the effort rubbed her skin until it became raw. By the time she moved it a half-inch, the abrasion on her nose felt like someone had taken a rasp to it, but she continued through the pain, through a mix of tears and fear, until each time, each millimeter, she created an even larger opening in the zipper.

She paused and placed her eye to the hole. Blinking, trying to focus on something within her dark shell, Roberta could make out tiny rays of light piercing the interior of the trunk.

She remembered similar rays of light like through holes in clouds after the rain. Jesus Rays, she called them—Jesus Rays.

Wrestling harder against the zipper, she dug open an even larger hole—a hole big enough to get her chin through. But she knew not to move too violently, or else the noose around her neck would tighten again.

Stopping from exhaustion, she started to whimper, but then she thought about the Jesus Rays. She sniffled until her tears stopped and then began to pray.

****

The old woman stopped once before looking down and setting her right foot onto the blacktop of the parking lot and continuing on her path to the garden area. When she looked up again, Mrs. Reynolds saw her target, the wooden slatted bench under the gazebo. It looked amazingly inviting to her, set off among all the wispy, pink and white petunias and red, curly geraniums.

Still, the cloudy sky worried her. She halted her forward motion and leaned, using the umbrella like a cane to hold herself up. Putting her other hand out, checking the weather, she determined rain might hold off long enough for her to sit outside a while and enjoy the outdoors.

Mrs. Reynolds had never minded the rain. It was only water. Her years had taught her as much. Also, water evaporates. If she got a little wet, she knew she would dry. Plus, she had her umbrella.

Chapter 23

"Phoenix, that's what he said." Biggs worried about Pinzer's decision on going back but didn't let Tanner get a whiff of his doubt.

"Dammit, Boss. You'd think he'd send us somewhere...unrelated." Tanner tapped his foot nervously on the floorboard.

"We do as he says."

"Let me talk to him. It sounds crazy. Phoenix is high-risk territory. We should go north. Let me ask him."

"He doesn't know you. Pinzer and I have history. I won't tell you again. He deals with me. And he says Phoenix."

Biggs turned the key and rolled down his window. A blast of rain-filled air washed over his face, and he realized he was sweating. He wiped his brow. When he brought his hand down, he wiped the moisture off onto his pants and reached into his pocket. He pulled out a paper towel and blotted his face.

"Turn on the air, Biggs." Tanner's voice grated.

Hawthorne glared back.

"You're disgusting. You're sweating like a pig."

Biggs dropped the towel and flung his heavy right arm out, flat-handing Tanner in the chest, thumping him with a crushing force enough to make him convulse under the weight of his blow.

"Listen, you little prick. I'm not going to tell you again. Pinzer deals with me. Only! Get over yourself."

Sucking air back into his lungs, Tanner coughed and grabbed at the front of his shirt.

Biggs flipped on the cooler, making the old car fizzle and spit out a slow stream of air.

"Piece of crap car," Tanner whined.

Biggs rolled his eyes as he turned up the window and strapped the seatbelt over his lap. He grabbed hold of the steering wheel gearshift, shoving the stick into reverse. He twisted his head to look behind him. Pressing slowly onto the gas, he watched the old woman he'd ridden down in the elevator with ambling out from under the lobby canopy, performing a shaky balancing act with her umbrella. When she stopped, her head tipped upward, and her hand leaned out as if trying to catch a drop of rain. Then she continued out into the lane.

****

They had not yet pulled out when Georgette's car inched into the front parking lot of the hotel. She nudged the car forward, noticing several cars; she counted five. The cars put up a barrier between her and Biggs's beige sedan.

Georgette depressed the brake with such slow, consistent pressure, she could barely feel the car come to a stop. She slid lower into her seat, hoping they hadn't seen her. She couldn't imagine they had. Their car was tucked into the parking space. But she couldn't be sure.

A clap of thunder resounded in the east, and the dark clouds appeared like a huge charcoal jellyfish in the sky with one million tentacles trailing underneath it.

God had spoken, and the heavens had opened up. Sunnydale would get hit within the half hour, maybe less.

The storm was an angry ram headed antlers down into a frontal assault with her town.

The rear lights of their car fluttered on, but the car remained parked. When she saw the driver's window open, Georgette sank down even lower in her seat, to the point where she had to peek through the steering wheel to see. And, through the prism of car windows between them, she could see some movement of Biggs's head but not much more.

Her heart beat thick in her chest, and when she licked her lips, she suddenly became aware of how stiff and dry her tongue was. She swallowed hard and could feel a glimmer of pasty moisture returning to her gums. She swallowed again, washing more saliva into her mouth.

Taking a deep breath in, she exhaled slowly. Her heart pounded. The palms of her hands felt sweaty, and she noticed her fingers shaking, so she clutched the steering wheel hard in an attempt to stop them.

With her eyes locked on the car, she hadn't noticed the old woman step onto the pavement.

A single drop of rain splattered the windshield in front of Georgette's eyes, skewing her vision around the splash. Then, as if a harbinger of what was to come, hundreds dribbled from somewhere above in a light sprinkle onto the glass, then, suddenly, thousands, tens of thousands of drops fell.

She adjusted the wiper mechanism to intermittent. It wasn't but a second or two until she had to crank up the speed on the wiper again. Rain was sluicing down the windshield, completely distorting her view of Biggs's car.

But when she saw his reverse beams light up and the car nudge back out of the parking space, she knew she would lose them if she didn't do something right now.

It was her only chance to stop them.

Georgette pressed hard onto the gas pedal, making the tires spin without traction. Then, after finally grabbing hold, the tires made the car lurch forward, like a bobcat after a rabbit.

They squirreled and lost traction again, sending the car into a hydroplane over the wet, dark pavement, making the rear of her car swing out and back in again, fishtailing and jostling Georgette around inside. She grabbed hard onto the steering wheel, trying to control her wild car with her eyes still locked onto Biggs.

She didn't see the old woman step in front of her.

****

An umbrella popped open. It reminded Georgette of a parachute opening behind one of those Formula race cars.

She yanked the steering wheel hard to the left. Skidding over a glassy layer of water and losing control, she felt her car shift and slide toward the row of parked cars on her left, trying to avoid the old woman walking behind the large, black parasol.

Just inches from hitting her, Georgette's car was in a spin.

Tires screamed out a warning for anyone nearby to hear—definitely to the woman who had now pulled her umbrella down stiff in front of her as she reacted to the shrill noise.

But then, the eeriest thing happened. Time slowed down to a nauseating pace.

The umbrella dropped out of the woman's hands, a fluttering pendulum wafting in slow motion to the wet, black ground, filling up with rainwater.

Georgette noticed the woman's face first—an ancient face. They stared at each other open-eyed, fear pasted to their skins. Each woman not feeling like they were reacting, but each only able to react—instinct had taken over.

The woman looked like an antique actress on a movie set, just out for a stroll on a gray, dismal day. Georgette imagined the set for a horror movie. Perhaps, a Hitchcock film.

It was queer to Georgette, sensing everything vividly but not being able to do anything but spin.

Teacups. She thought of the circus ride and wanted to vomit.

The old woman stumbled backward. Had Georgette hit her?

The woman spun toward the lobby's cabana, catching herself with the cane and limping finally to a column where she clutched onto it as if she were hiding next to it.

No, Georgette didn't think she'd hit her, but she wasn't sure.

She noticed a bellhop from inside race out to her aid, but as she passed, she lost track of them both.

Georgette's car felt like an E-ticket ride, like the whirling bowls she'd ridden on at the fair as a child. Teacups, shifting you one way and then the other, swinging her torso out of rhythm as the car skidded.

The sudden crushing stop jarred Georgette's head

forward, thumping it once against the steering wheel. The white balloon from the airbag exploded, inhaling and exhaling, emptying, then hanging off the steering column like a used rubber. It all happened in a matter of seconds. All of it.

When she looked up, her car was on top of Biggs's car. She'd collided into the rear driver side bumper of their vehicle, crushing the trunk, pleating its hatch ajar but pinching it tighter all in one motion.

She unbuckled her seat belt. Tanner flung open his door. Georgette opened hers.

Stepping up for action, Tanner left his passenger door fully open, and in one swift action, he pulled out his gun and fired into the old car's steel shell.

Pumping one, two, three shots into it, crossways but near the rear. The *tink tink tink* resonated, each pellet resounding and muffled fast under the crashing rush of rain.

Georgette's legs buckled, leaving her behind her car door for cover. Her body began to shake wildly. Rain slid off her dry hair onto her face, making her blink, trying to see. Her hands felt for her waistband. She grabbed the flare gun double-fisted, trying to control it. A crack of thunder blasted, making her dip down further behind her door.

"Martin!" She spoke, not believing she would've called attention to herself but somehow understanding why. Someone was in the trunk who Tanner wanted dead. Someone. And she knew who the *someone* was. It was Roberta.

He popped off two more shots. *Tink tink.*

She waved one hand out past the cover of her car door. Then poked her head out. He held a gun, a .38, her .38, sideways, like a rookie gangbanger.

"Martin! Stop shooting."

"Screw you, bitch!" He stopped for a second, then laughed at his own comment.

She stood up enough to see out through the window at him but ducked down again.

"Martin. Now hold up here just a sec, will you?" She shoved her flare gun into her pants again and stood up again, very slowly.

His smile worried her, but he dropped the arm he was wielding and the gun to his side. "What!"

A distant siren whined, screaming its arrival. "Hear that, Martin?" She held her hands up in surrender, showing him she had no weapon.

He nodded. "Yeah, I hear it."

The beige sedan's driver-side door opened, and Biggs rolled out onto the ground. Georgette's eyes flitted between Tanner and Biggs, who was now crawling along the ground in front of the row of parked vehicles.

Tanner, still nodding, continued. "You know what it means?"

Georgette shifted between the cover of the door, then fully out in the open, to Tanner, then back behind the door again, trying to see where Biggs went. She felt a cold sweat rush over her, like the cosmos was sending a message.

She shifted behind the door again and looked behind her. She saw Biggs running toward the rear of the hotel. Georgette pulled out the flare gun without Tanner noticing.

Bringing her attention back to Tanner, she answered, "No, Martin. What does it mean?"

"It means..." he smiled again, chuckling like someone had made a joke. Then he dropped his arm, egging her on, "Now, why are you hiding? Come on out, Georgette, where I can see you."

She moved slowly, inching tight against the door, holding her left arm up and her right down, with the flare gun behind the door. "I'm here. Now, Martin, what can I do for you?" Her voice sounded freakishly calm, unnerving Tanner.

He jerked and lifted his gun in a blink.

Instantly, she sprung sideways toward the parked cars. Closing her eyes, she fired.

He fired.

The bullet whizzed past her right ear.

The flare's comet waggled out directly at him. She rolled onto and off the car next to the sedan, banging her shoulder in the process.

Tanner's face froze.

The burning torch arched and dipped on its trail over the crumpled trunk and landed directly into the front of his pants, sticking there like a smoldering cigarette, burning a hole into his jeans at the crotch. He buckled backward.

He'd shot his last bullet.

Chapter 24

Georgette had three more flares in her pockets.
She loaded another one.

Rain drenched the scene, but the flare burned bright, scorching Tanner's pants as he tried to knock it off but not wanting to touch it all at the same time. He roared out in pain, batting at the fire stick as it melted into him. He ran in a circle, trying to douse it. But the explosive material of the flare had a burn time of no less than fifteen minutes. And Tanner's penis would never last ablaze for fifteen minutes. He had to get it off somehow. He fell to the ground, writhing in pain.

With him busy with his own set of problems, Georgette lost interest in him.

She pounded her fists onto the trunk and screamed, "Roberta!" Hearing nothing, her breathing took on panic. She wedged her fingers under the rim of the trunk and tried to lift, but the crumpled metal had bent and locked the lid into place. She pounded again. "Roberta!" Her voice splintering into shards, she sobbed. "Help! Someone help!"

At first, she heard movement, shuffling inside. Then she heard Roberta's weak voice. "I'm okay."

"Roberta? Are you hit?"

The muffled voice folded into the thick wall of the trunk, muffled through a slice between the car's bumper and the hood.

"I can't hear you!" Georgette shrieked.

"I don't think so." The voice came through louder this time with instructions, "Go get that son of a bitch, George."

"What about you?"

"Go!"

Georgette looked over where Tanner lay, moaning in anguish. He could die there.

Then she looked to her left in the direction Hawthorne had run. She patted at her pockets for something to write with. Nothing.

She ran back to her car and found a marker in the console.

Back at the trunk, she scrawled on top of the hood, "*Willy! Roberta is in here!!!*"

"The police are coming, Rob!"

"George, go!"

Georgette patted the top of the hood but didn't wait around.

She leaped into a sprint.

She needed to confront Hawthorne.

****

Hawthorne had shimmied down the twenty-foot sloping wall into the gully a few yards behind his truck. A trail of fresh mud trailed down toward his descent. It oozed like lava.

He brushed off the back of his denims from sliding on his ass on the way down. A layer of mud caked his hands.

Georgette caught a glimpse of Hawthorne's large figure dive low and disappear in between the hedge's planting of oleanders and some tall evergreens growing along the edge of the canal, about a hundred yards ahead of her.

She held her flare gun up to her chest and shuffled over to the hedge with her back against it, hiding among the green, speared leaves. Each movement washed rainwater off the hedge's leaves and onto her. Rain had completely soaked her clothing and matted her hair into a snarl of peach-stained curls, ripe peaches. Her blouse clung to her and showed every tight muscle, every curve, as she slinked along the same path to the point where Biggs ducked out of sight.

Sirens howled close now, probably on hotel property, from what she could determine by their noise. Mud lay thick and deep along the riverside, its gritty smell reminding her of a more innocent time when she had made muddies as a kid.

Rolling thunder skipped behind her, nearly tapping her shoulder. The electrical show had moved in too close. Lightning tracers arced and flashed behind her, setting off the landscape like an enormous spotlight, bringing every living thing into view.

Peering through the hedge, the gully's basin was muddy and wet, but a flash flood had not yet made its way much farther west.

She heard a quick *blip blip* of his truck's remote unlocking the doors.

"Hawthorne!" She screamed through the pouring rain as she appeared on the river side of the hedge. He stood below her at his truck down in the riverbed. He hadn't opened the door yet. He was just standing there, looking at her. She could see his steely eyes even from the distance separating them.

"What in hell do you want, Georgette?"

"A few answers might be nice."

"Answers? What answers?"

"Like why, Hawthorne. Why?"

"Why do you think?"

She shrugged her shoulders, holding the flare gun in her right hand and shaking her head, then dropping her arms in a pathetic gesture.

"Cash. Why else. Money. Cash, Georgette."

Not seeing a weapon on him, she walked closer along the edge of the river.

A huge rush of thunder slammed closer, and another sheet of rain cut across the sky like a rudder, ever closer, skipping off the hardened earth and skimming the ground, etching a path much the way the earth had been formed millions of years ago, like the Grand Canyon.

She looked down and noticed trickling water flowing into the mud veins of the dark wet gully, cresting, overflowing, and building.

"Hawthorne. You need to come up here."

"Georgette, there's nothing you can do."

They were yelling, but the wind and rain, and thunder consumed their voices. She wasn't sure if he could hear her. She yelled louder. Cupping her hands to her mouth, she remembered she was holding what looked like a gun.

"No, Hawthorne. Come up here with me!"

"Georgette. It's over with us!"

She couldn't believe his words and dropped her hands back down. He must have thought she wanted him back. She cocked her head and then shook it.

"No!" She tried to scream her words, "That's not what I mean!" Something was crashing in the distance, making it impossible to be heard.

"You were just a means to an end." At once, she understood everything.

Her hand gripped the flare gun tight. Her face pinched in anger, and the water began running like a shallow creek.

"No, you idiot. Come up here where it's safe!"

But, in a second, a clap, the sound of two planks of wood crashed. A tree snapped and fell behind her. It shrieked like the sudden bark of a large hound, making Georgette duck. Then the sound electrified, sounding like sheets of glass crashing against concrete.

She dropped to her knees, covering her head with her arms. When nothing landed on her, she figured she was safe. She was in no immediate danger of being hit by the falling tree.

But Hawthorne...

She turned and looked back.

A wall of water filling the river bed halfway up its berm, a good ten feet high or so, had snaked its way into view and was tumbling straight for his truck. She screamed. "Get out! Get out!" And pointed in the direction of the tsunami headed for him.

Seeing the water raging toward him, he turned, scrambled to the side of the gully, and tried to crawl back up to higher ground.

But the rain had muddied only a thin layer of earth, leaving looser dirt beneath it, making him slide back down to the bottom of the berm again.

"Hawthorne, get out!" she screamed again, seeing the panic in his eyes.

She reached out to him, and he moved forward as if to grab her hand, but when he looked at the water barreling toward him, he turned and ran to the truck. He flung the door open and closed it again just before the wall of water hit.

It was acrobatic, the way it lifted the truck like a toy, tumbling it up, flipping it end over end, then rolling it onto its side over and over, washing it down the river, bobbing it up, dropping it under, and continuing its assault until the water pushed Hawthorne around a bend and out of sight.

"No!" Georgette crumpled to her knees, screaming until the air in her lungs wouldn't let her scream any longer, until her tears bleached the word "no" into shadows, into two ghosts of letters, until her crying took on no sound at all, until she lost her breath.

And when she breathed, she began the process all over again, slumped over her knees in the mud by the river as the water rushed by below her, stealing everything living within the crevice into its current.

Chapter 25

The flare rose high. Like a lone shooting star, it pierced the cloudy day as it rose higher, higher than the hotel's roofline, higher than the old Ponderosa pine trees surrounding the waterway.

Sounds of rushing water continued tumbling around her. Straggled, wet strands of hair covered her face. Tears intermixed with rain washed off her nose into the soggy earth next to the torrent, crashing, racing, boiling past. Its reverberation, its din masked Willy's car racing up behind her, next to her, skidding to a stop on the asphalt.

She only heard him approach, the welcome sound of a human being. He ran to her. Cupping his body over hers, Willy held Georgette tight. The warmth of his body let her know how cold the rain had made her, and she shivered, finally remembering she was alive.

"Georgette, I thought I'd lost you." His grip tightened around her. She wondered how it was possible, but he managed to pull her even closer to him, there on the wet ground by the raging river. "When I saw the water coming, we were still prying open the trunk."

"Roberta!" His words broke the stupor she had sunk into.

"Is she…" Georgette covered her mouth with one hand.

"She'll be fine, but she's pretty beat up."

"Oh, that's good, Willy. That's good." Pushing off the ground, Willy backed away but only by inches. She brushed her pants and smeared mud across her legs and down her butt. Noticing mud had soiled her arms up to her elbows, she said, "I need to see her."

"Let's go. Before they take her."

He put out a hand to help her off the mound, and she stepped down to the pavement. Pulling her hand back, she stopped. "Hawthorne…"

But Willy shushed her. He stepped back to where she had stopped and led her to the passenger door. She was shivering. "You're cold."

"Funny thing, I don't feel cold. I'm just shaking like a leaf all of the sudden."

"Yeah, George, that's called shock. Let's get you inside the car."

Inside, he reached across her body and pulled the seatbelt over her, locking the harness into place with a snap. "There." He patted her mud-caked arm. "How's that?"

"Good. Thanks, Willy." She didn't quite get why he needed to strap her in, they were only driving around the hotel, but she let him. He needed to help her, so she let him.

"I'll kick on the heater. That will help too. I'm sure the EMTs have some thermal blankets."

"Oh, Lord, Willy. I'm fine." But as the words came out, her body did a double-step on shivering. "Good gravy. What's happening to me?"

"Like I said, Georgie," he flipped the gear into drive, "it's called shock."

Roberta sat on the bumper of an ambulance. A

second ambulance had just carted Tanner into it, closed the doors, and rushed off with its lights blaring and sirens howling.

One of the EMTs, a big man, a young Pakistani who looked a lot like a doctor, kept busy checking Roberta's vitals. The other, a blonde, slight young woman with a running weight of no more than one hundred pounds—what Georgette could tell from her puny size—covered Roberta with a thermal wrap. It shone like a silver cape around her shoulders.

Willy's car had barely come to a stop when Georgette unbuckled her belt and opened the door. Willy rolled his eyes, stopping short and abruptly for her to exit safely.

Georgette, in a full pace, ran to Roberta.

When Roberta saw Georgette coming, she smiled. "George!" She stood and limped, hobbling her way over to Georgette.

When Georgette reached her, she grabbed her hard and held her tight. "Roberta," her voice shattered.

"George." Roberta hid her beaten and swollen face in Georgette's neck.

She felt Roberta's body tighten, then relax as she cried openly.

"It's okay. You're safe now." Roberta buried her head against Georgette's shoulder and moaned a low, sad sound reminding Georgette of a dying fawn, a bleak sound.

"I kept praying, you know, George, to God. Praying hard, like never before." She paused, breathing in short, choppy breaths, and continued, "Then I heard them. You know, the ancients, George. They whispered to me." Georgette clutched her harder. "At my blackest moment, I heard them calling to me, calling my name." Her next words quivered out in a whisper. "I swear."

"Shhh. Shhh."

The two women stood there in the parking lot together while Willy and the EMTs watched. Car radios scratched on and off in the background, sending messages to anyone who might be listening, but no one was. Red and white lights whipped around in a constant spin, alternating in color on top of Roberta's ambulance. It was almost like someone muted the volume on a commercial while everyone waited for action to resume.

Roberta sniffled first, pulling back and bringing her sleeve up to wipe her nose. "I need a tissue," she whispered to Georgette, smiling meekly.

"She needs a tissue." Georgette turned and spoke.

Roberta's nose was bleeding inside and out. Her left eye had swollen to a mere slit where her eyelashes met. The hematoma caused her eye to puff out. It looked raw and pink around a gash over her eyebrow. Her upper and lower lips had gashes and were blue from bruising.

Someone draped one of the shiny silver thermal blankets over Georgette's shoulders. She hardly noticed. They appeared like a caped team standing there together.

"She needs a tissue!" Georgette yelled again, looking around the others at the scene. Everyone jumped to life again, running around and looking in places where they thought they might find a tissue. It was Willy, however, who walked up behind them and offered his handkerchief.

Roberta took it and wiped, forgetting about the tear

on the end of her nose. She winced but dabbed again, this time lightly. "Thank you, Willy."

Georgette turned back to Roberta and chuckled silently to her. "You probably could have whatever you want if you asked right now."

"You know what I really want?" Her right eye got moist along the inside rim of her lower lid, and her left eye seeped out tears.

"What's that, honey?" Georgette pulled Roberta's hands up together into hers.

"Some of your coffee." Her shoulders made tiny jerks as she started to cry. "I kept thinking…"

"Shhh, it's okay."

"I kept thinking, *'If I get out of this alive, I would love to sit and have some of Georgette's coffee with her.'* "

"Like I said, anything, sweetie. Anything you want, you got." She pulled Roberta back into a hug. "You know what sounds better than my coffee, Rob?" She pulled out of the clutch again.

"Hmm." As Roberta wiped at the tears in her eyes, Georgette noticed how her hands were shaking and how bruises covered her knuckles too.

"That cruise." Georgette let go and led Roberta back to the bumper for her to sit down. As they walked, she continued, "What do you say we both take that cruise together?"

"Sounds wonderful. I wonder if Rick would mind."

"He can come too. My treat. We'll have a ball.

"Anyway, we could all use a break."

"Where is he, George? Does Rick know about any of this? Is he still in Laughlin?"

"I don't know, honey." She looked at Willy. "Do

201

you know?"

"We'll contact him as soon as we get statements from you and Tanner."

She had somehow forgotten about Tanner. Hearing his name made Georgette growl, "Tanner. I'd nearly forgotten. It's easy how a person can sidestep a piece of crap like him."

Roberta reached out with her hand, grabbing Georgette's arm. "What happened to Hawthorne?"

Georgette looked down. A sudden lump in her throat caused her to whisper. "He..." She shook her head, turning away toward the road, away from their faces.

"They were going to kill me, George."

"I know." She turned back. "I know. It just seems so surreal. Like we stepped off a cliff and are still falling. I just can't believe any of it."

"We have to get the mayor to the hospital. That nose looks bad," the male EMT ordered. His nametag read *SHANN*.

Georgette turned her head so he couldn't see her tears, nodding for them to take Roberta. "Willy, can you take me to the hospital too?"

"Anything, Georgie. Anything for you."

Looking up at him, she smiled. Then, turning to Roberta, she winked tears from her eyes, making a joke. "Anything? Well, aren't I special?" The male EMT helped Roberta up by the elbow and guided her into the back of the ambulance. "I'll be right behind you," Georgette reassured her.

"We'll be right behind you," Willy corrected her.

"We." Georgette nodded quickly, keeping her eyes on Roberta as they closed the door of the ambulance, walking to remain in view until they finally closed and locked the door and she could see Roberta no longer.

She patted a flat hand on the window and yelled through the doors, "We'll be right behind you!"

Georgette heard Roberta's answer, now muffled by the wall between them, as she yelled back, "I love you!"

****

As Georgette and Willy watched from a clubhouse window, the excavator with its sawtooth bucket dug up chunk after chunk of soil, starting at hole number one of the golf course. They watched in a sunny spot through the plate glass window. A sky like someone had thrown a bucket of robin's egg blue paint across it could be seen well past the foothills, well past the rolling green mounds of the golf course.

Not a cloud was in sight. The days since the flood had played out a more typical fashion for Arizona, with days sunny and warm and with clear skies.

"You can use the driving range. We're not doing anything to it." Jeff, the pro, looked at them as he waited for their decision.

"Want to just hit some balls?"

"Sure." Georgette smiled at Willy. "I don't know if I could do a whole round of golf anyway."

"Okay. We'll take some tokens and a golf cart."

"How many tokens you want?"

"Enough for five large buckets each."

"That'll be fifty dollars for the tokens and another fifteen for the cart."

He fished in his pocket for the money, pulled out a stack of folded bills, and flipped through, counting off twenty, forty, then sixty, and eighty. "There you go."

Jeff gave Willy fifteen dollars back in change and ten tokens. Willy turned to Georgette and counted off five tokens, dropping each in the palm of her hand.

"I'll get your cart." He walked past them and out the door. Georgette and Willy walked a few steps behind Jeff and stopped in the gravel lot where they would receive the golf cart. The scent of freshly dug earth hung heavy in the air.

"You can use my seven iron."

"Okay." She smiled at him.

"You okay?"

"Oh, I'm fine. Just not quite used to the thought of you and me. That's all."

"Well, missy," he faked a John Wayne accent. "Get used to it."

She giggled at his impersonation.

"Pretty good, huh?"

"Not really, Will. I'm giggling at you."

He grabbed her around the waist, swung her around, and kissed her. His tongue felt warm and soft. He kissed so nice.

They heard the buzz of the golf cart and the crunching of its tires on the gravel as it pulled off the paved road and onto the pebbled lot where they stood. Willy pulled back but leaned in quick once more and kissed her softly on the lips.

"Here. Let me get those for you." Jeff grabbed Willy's clubs and put them in the back of the cart. "You know where it is, right, Willy?"

"I certainly do, Jeff. Thanks."

"Have fun, you two." Jeff saluted and turned back to go to the pro shop.

"Wanna drive?"

"No! I don't know how to drive one of these things."

"It's easy. I'll show you."

He pressed the foot pedal, and they started off with a jolt, bumping along the cart path toward the driving range some six hundred yards from the clubhouse. Georgette craned her neck to watch the excavator.

"That's the hole, isn't it?"

"Yeah, but honey, I don't see Tanner's, Taggert's—whatever the hell his name was—statements as being very credible. He went off the tomato truck after getting his unit fried into a tater tot."

"Willy!"

"Well, what would you call it?"

"I'd call it a tragedy." She meant everything up to now that had happened.

"He went nuts, George."

She measured out how she wanted to say the next words. "I know these were bad men and all, Willy, but everything that's happened is really sad to me." Georgette paused. "What happened to Roberta, of course, but also what happened to them, to Hawthorne. Tanner, too, I guess..." Her words trailed off when Willy spoke up.

"They were stone-cold killers. If their plan had worked, your Biggs fellow would've married you, then killed you too."

From his peripheral vision, he could see she was shaking her head. "It's so freaky. It seems so impossible."

"Well, it's over now." They neared the driving range. He depressed the small brake, and the little cart came to a stop near the empty driving range. Willy never understood how, on such a beautiful day like this day, people never seemed to get out. "Here we are."

"Hey, Willy?"

"Mm-hmm." He had jumped out and was pulling his golf bag out of the cart and walking over to the first two-man mesh enclosure for the shade shelter.

"Can we play golf on the cruise ship, you think?"

"Oh, absolutely!" He turned back and smiled at her. "Does Roberta know how to golf?"

"I think she has before, but I'm not sure how much."

"What day are we leaving again, George? Did you say June twelfth?"

"That's right. Why? Is that too far into the future for you, Willy? Too much of a commitment?"

"Come here, you sweet woman, and address the ball." He held out a club for her.

"This the seven?"

"Yep."

She looked down at the ball. "Ball, I'm going to hit you now." She looked at Willy and beamed out a smile at him. "How's that for addressing the ball?"

"Nice."

She wiggled her rear as she stepped into place, angling the club down at the back of the golf ball.

"Nice," he repeated, noticing her rump moving. She wiggled again and poked her butt out more, taunting him.

"I'm gonna bite it if you do that again."

"That wouldn't be very sportsmanlike of you." She put a hand up to shield her eyes from the sun. "Okay. I'm not foolin' around now." She steadied her footing, looked out at the one hundred-yard marker, then back down at the ball. She pulled her arms in a nice even backstroke the way Jeff had taught her and swung down, hitting the ball square on the club's sweet spot. It soared out past one hundred yards, about twenty-five feet or so. She screamed and jumped up and down. "I hit it, Willy! I hit it!"

"Good Lord, George. That was beautiful. Now do it again."

"What say we call it good and go home? I mean, it can only go downhill from here."

"You're crazy, you know that?"

Chapter 26

The four of them waved at people below on the boardwalk.

The last few people boarded, walking up the gangplank, everyone looking like they were straight out of a yacht club. All sailors in their own right, playing parts.

A warm, coastal June air swept up and onto the deck where they stood. Feeling a muggy layer on her skin, she wiped her forearm. It felt cool and warm all at the same time. The sun felt hot on the tender skin of her chest. The dress she wore revealed her cleavage from its low scooping neckline. She had splurged on Saks.com, spending a small fortune on four special dresses, the chocolate-colored polka dot one she wore today and three others she intended to wear for special occasions on their one-week journey to Aruba.

As the four of them gazed out, Georgette focused on the colors of Port Everglades. Florida was pretty with its pink buildings and squat, feathery palm trees intermixed with tall Queen palms hovering over the land. She wondered which ones produced dates or if any did.

She thought how funny it was how the green brackish water she peered down into now had appeared blue from a distance, how the water could draw you in closer with a blue oasis, but then how it showed its true identity close up, kind of like people.

She closed her eyes, soaking in the warmth.

"Georgette! I can't believe we're doing this, just leaving the diner high and dry!" Roberta giggled out.

"Cammy knows what to do. Plus, she just thinks she's died and gone to heaven since we promoted her to manager."

"Yeah, well, she deserves it. She's a natural."

Georgette took in a long draw of fresh air. Ocean air had a smell she missed from when she lived near the west coast. A mix of fish and wet sand, of kelp and campfires, always took her back to the first time she'd ever seen the ocean as a young woman working in the Bay Area in a crusty little bar—the place she left before heading south to Arizona. It was funny to her how she always thought she could never leave a place near water, and now she felt she wouldn't ever want to leave the desert.

They stood silently, still waving at people one hundred feet below the liner on the deck, at people waving back, at people they didn't know.

"There are lots of stripes down there. Lots of white hats, sandals, and stripes."

"Beach fashion." Roberta dropped her hand and turned to Georgette. "By the way, you look smashing in that sundress, George." She looked straight at her chest, then whispered behind her hand, "Your boobs! They're huge!" Her eye was still a little swollen, but Roberta had done a great job with makeup to hide the residual bruising. Her lips would probably be forever scarred but it sort of looked pretty on her.

"Shut up!" The guys were in their own little world, not paying too much attention until Georgette screamed and laughed at Roberta.

"What's that?" Willy smiled, finally looking over to Georgette.

"Well, Willy," Roberta started, "I was just commenting on Georgette's dress."

"Okay. Okay." She put her hand up to Roberta's lips. "Don't you dare."

"Girl stuff, Willy." Rick shrugged his shoulders and walked over to his wife.

"Honey, what do you say, we go get an adult refreshment?"

"Lovely, dear. Sounds lovely." Rick put his hand on his wife's back and guided her away. "We'll meet you in the cocktail lounge?"

"Sure!" Willy chimed in before Georgette, who nodded and smiled.

The ship bellowed out a long honk of a foghorn, alerting people they were about to shove off.

"Shall we, dear?" Willy gestured with one arm in the direction of Roberta and Rick.

"Absolutely." Georgette turned to pick up her big straw tote bag sitting next to her foot on the deck. She didn't notice the man there all clad in platinum white—white jacket, white pants, white shoes, and even a white hat, a felt trilby.

As they stepped out onto the deck, the white man clipped her elbow, knocking her hard into the starboard railing.

"Oh, my!" She barely caught herself against the metal bar rail.

"Excuse me, ma'am." He tipped his hat.

Recovering from the railing, she replied. "Not a problem. I must've stepped into you."

"Hey, buddy." Willy immediately got angry, stepping in toward the man.

"It was an accident, Willy." She pulled his arm back into her. "It's okay."

"Only an accident. My apologies, ma'am." His sharp black eyes danced between them, and Georgette thought she recognized him.

"Do I know—" But before she could ask, he sauntered off, tipping his white hat again.

"The rude bastard."

"Willy. He apologized. It was just an accident."

"You okay?"

"Of course, Willy. It was just a bump."

He grabbed the arm she fell on. As Willy checked Georgette, she looked over her shoulder to find the man who she thought had been looking in their direction too. But then he disappeared among a throng of other passengers, and she lost sight of him.

"Oh, honey. I'm fine. Let's go find Rob and Rick."

She picked up her bag and hooked her arm in Willy's. They headed toward the cocktail lounge but really, they were headed into a new adventure.

Chapter 27

"What's this guy's name again?"

"Melvin Taggert, AKA Martin Tanner." Caimen rubbed a hand over the tiny pin curls of his hair. Specks of gray were beginning to betray him, giving away his age, about mid-forty, Pinzer figured.

"No, can't say that I have ever heard of him." It was true. He had never heard of anyone named Melvin Taggert, or if he thought about it, Martin Tanner.

Pinzer sat back against the cool metal frame of the chair and crossed his legs, adjusting the pant leg of his government-issued orange overalls and sliding the chair back a few inches in the process. The caged room echoed as the chair grated over the concrete floor. He stared across the faux marble table at Assistant District Attorney Clark Caimen, who looked two beats away from heart failure.

Pinzer held his manacled hands loosely in his lap and interlocked his fingers.

"He says you hired him." Caimen adjusted his round, wire-framed glasses, pushing them up the bridge of his nose. A tell to Pinzer.

"News to me." He looked over to his lawyer, who shrugged.

"Look, he answered you. He doesn't know Mr. Taggert. What kind of evidence do you have, Mr. Caimen?" Ruckheimer, Pinzer's lawyer, chimed in.

"This guy's testimony."

"Again, sir, do you have any evidence linking Taggert to my client, any corroborating evidence?" Ruckheimer set his tone, pressing Caimen.

"Says you hired a certain Mr. Hawthorne Biggs." Caimen looked away from Ruckheimer and back to Pinzer for the answer.

"I never hired any Hawthorne Biggs." Pinzer sniggered. Tweeter, Pinzer's henchman from before, had hired some guy, and he figured Biggs was his alias, but he wasn't about to offer the information to the ADA.

"This guy says a lot of things, I hear. Sounds like the man has lost it. Spewing some craziness about a golf course, about some evidence there, while at the same time pointing the finger here at this innocent man." Ruckheimer indicated Pinzer, who tipped his head to the side, trying to look the part. "Isn't this Taggert being held, as we speak, at the Arizona State Hospital? For observation? Really, counselor. Is this the best witness you have?"

Ruckheimer leaned in, whispering into Pinzer's ear. Pinzer pulled back and stared at him, no more than two inches from Ruckheimer. Up so close to the man, the oil beading off the lawyer's nose looked like a slick. It flowed completely across his jowls and up over his waning hairline, which made a wide cay of skin on top of his head. He wouldn't have hired the guy if he'd seen him first. He came with recommendations. Heard he was the best. It didn't mean Pinzer had to like the guy. Before coming into the meeting, Ruckheimer must've had coffee and a cigarette. A clear ashtray scent rose off the greasy sweat covering his mouth. Pinzer closed the gap, getting closer to his ear with his lips, and whispered into the lawyer's ear. Then he pulled away and looked again at the ADA.

"My client knows no one by the name of Hawthorne Biggs and has nothing to offer, that is unless you do."

"We'll drop the current two years to eighteen months."

Ruckheimer smiled and dragged out a thin cloth from his chest pocket. He wiped it over his mouth, around his nose, and quickly around, making two circles covering his entire face. "So, we're gonna make a deal, are we?" Ruckheimer's smile broadened, and he leaned forward over the table, placing both hands flat on it. "Sounds like this Taggert guy is part of the investigation at this point. He has nothing to clear him except some fiction about my client's involvement."

The ADA didn't move. He looked like a mannequin sitting there, not flinching, hardly breathing, and waiting.

"Okay, Caimen. This is my offer. Time served, and he's out end of business tomorrow."

"Time served and six months."

"Time served, six months house arrest."

Caimen paused and looked at his watch. "We'll have the paperwork drawn up and to your office by the end of the week."

Ruckheimer countered. "By the end of business tomorrow."

"Deal. So spill it. How is Taggert involved?"

Pinzer's lawyer nodded to him. Pinzer sat forward. "This is just a guess, but if you do some checking, I bet Biggs isn't this guy's real name. Maybe it's short for something, maybe Biganski. I don't know. It's a guess, mind you. Maybe this Taggert fellow and he were involved, but, like I said, it's just a guess. I don't know them, nor have I ever met either one." He knew they had no evidence linking Biganski to him, or they would've caught up to him by now.

"Uh huh."

"Well, gentlemen." Ruckheimer slapped his beefy hands together, rubbing them hard as he looked back and forth between Pinzer and Caimen. "It's always a pleasure, counselor." A statement held out for the winning side, Ruckheimer slid back into his chair then slammed his fists onto the tabletop before standing and extending his hand to shake.

"Yes, well, the pleasure is mine." The words churned out of Caimen's lips. His eyes looked sullen and sour. He extended a limp arm and shook quickly, one pump down, and then released Ruckheimer. He had gotten nothing linking Biggs or Taggert to Pinzer.

"Tomorrow, then."

Caimen nodded at Ruckheimer, collected his briefcase, and called the guard to open the room.

Ruckheimer put a finger to his mouth to make sure Pinzer wouldn't say anything until he was gone.

"Actually, four o'clock would be better. We could expedite the release of my client by the end of the day."

The door swung open where a guard stood.

Caimen turned back and glared at Ruckheimer. "We'll see what we can do." With that, Caimen left.

"Please, my client and I have more work," Pinzer's lawyer told the guard. After the door closed again, he spoke. "You'll be out tomorrow, Zach." Ruckheimer, pleased with his performance, smiling wide, was always looking for approval from his clients.

It irked Zach.

"That's what I pay you for, Wallace. Try to remember that." Ruckheimer's smile dissolved into a slim line, one tracing the thinnest distinction between client and attorney confidentiality. "Yes, well. Shall I have a car come by to pick you up?"

"I've got it from here, Wallace."

"So, what's the first thing you'll do as a free man?" Ruckheimer asked more out of curiosity than because he cared about Pinzer.

"Well, Wallace, I hear the Caribbean is beautiful, especially Aruba." His right lip curled into a half-smile. "I'm thinking about taking a cruise." He turned and gazed through the room's only window, through its bars, past the cinder tarmac of the institutional parking lot, past the streetlights, past the city. He stared thousands of miles off to the ocean.

"You'll still be under house arrest, which means..." But Pinzer cut him off.

"I know what house arrest means, Wallace. My ankle bracelet will have GPS. It can't leave the house."

"It can't leave?" Ruckheimer glared at Pinzer. "I don't want to know any more of your plans, Zach. Just watch yourself." Understanding the meeting was over, Ruckheimer offered an open hand for Pinzer to shake, but Pinzer acted as if the shackles made it impossible for him to do so.

Ruckheimer snuck back his hand, dropping his arm to his side. Then he gathered his files and briefcase and called for the guard.

Pinzer had a plan for the ankle bracelet. He also had a needy girlfriend who would do anything for him.

She had pretty legs. The bracelet would look nice on her.

A word about the author...

Susan Wingate is a #1 Amazon bestseller and an award-winning author of books spanning a few fiction genres. Susan Wingate writes award-winning novels recommended for teenagers, young adults, and for older adults who are young at heart!

Susan lives on an island off the coast of Washington State with her husband Bob.

You can find Susan Wingate's other books at the following:

Susan's website: http://www.susanwingate.com

Amazon: https://amzn.to/2yplQVR

Barnes&Noble: http://www.barnesandnoble.com/c/susan-wingate

To keep up on Susan Wingate's activities, visit her at:

Facebook: http://www.facebook.com/authorsusanwingate

Twitter: http://www.twitter.com/susanwingate

LinkedIn: http://linked.com/in/susanwingate

Thank you for purchasing
this publication of The Wild Rose Press, Inc.

For questions or more information
contact us at
info@thewildrosepress.com.

The Wild Rose Press, Inc.
www.thewildrosepress.com